Whispers & Broken Promises

GRANITE COVE
BOOK FOUR

DENISE CARBO

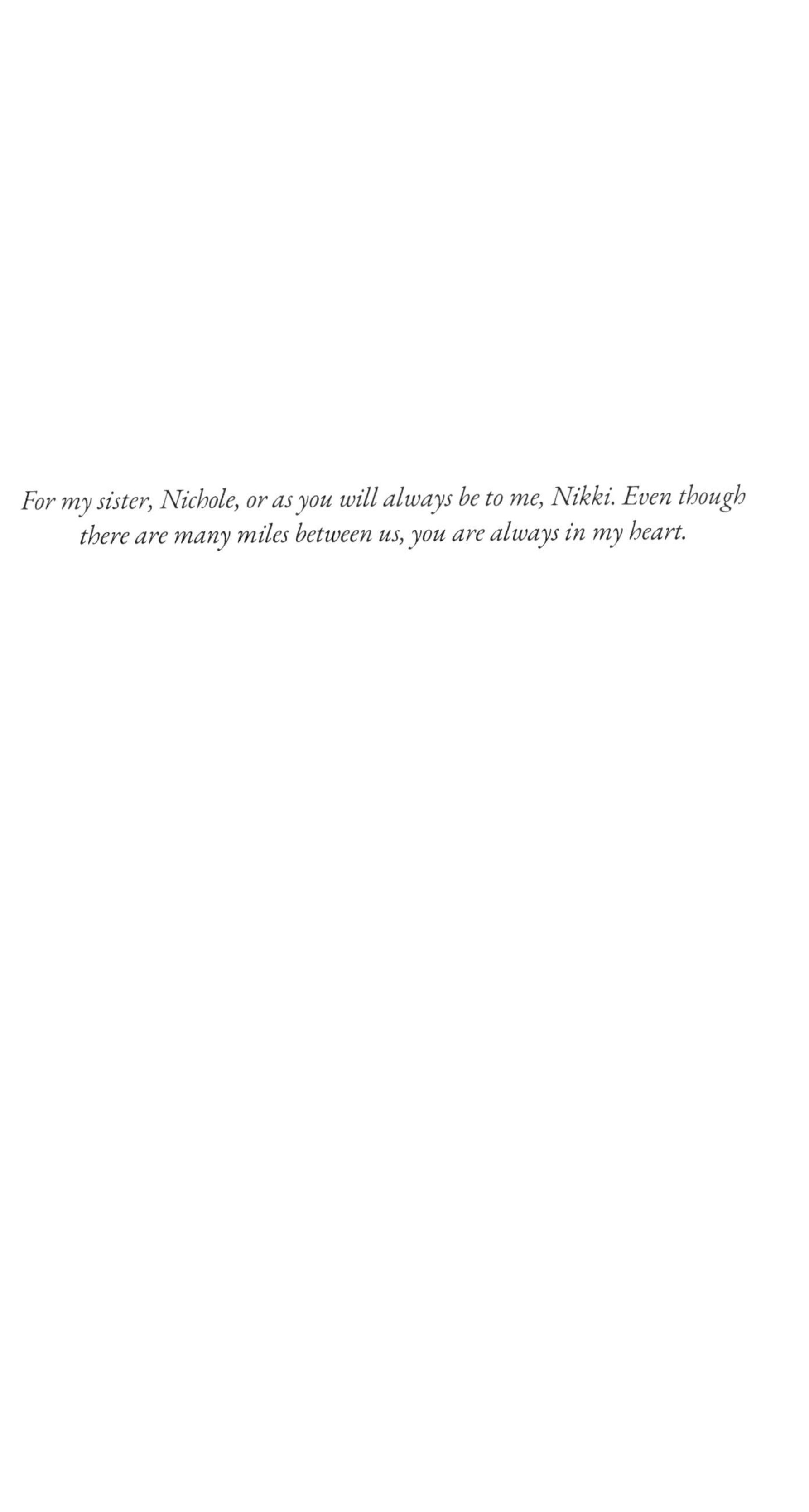

For my sister, Nichole, or as you will always be to me, Nikki. Even though there are many miles between us, you are always in my heart.

Preface

Whispers & Broken Promises takes place a few years before *My First My Last My Only*. This is Tina's story and the beginning of book club.

Chapter One

"I'm a good person." *Am I though?*

Jack didn't think so, and he was one of the people I thought knew me best. I finger the modest gold hoop earring in my ear while waiting for the stoplight to change to green.

"Getting a little revenge wouldn't make you a bad person." The sarcasm laden tone is classic Jen. If they handed out sarcasm awards, my sister would be the champion.

I picture Jen rolling her eyes while she presses her phone between her shoulder and cheek. From the background noise coming through the phone, she's probably in her bathroom getting ready for work. The running water and distinct echo of a small room are dead giveaways.

"Prank calling him at his new job or trolling him on social media is not my style." I may have fantasized about him getting fired or dumped a few dozen times over the past few weeks, but I didn't want to be instrumental in either of those things happening. No, I wanted them to happen because of his own actions. And suddenly, of course, he would realize I was the best thing to ever happen to him and he would beg me to accept him back.

I would listen to all his groveling and then send him on his way. I wouldn't take him back.

Probably.

Okay, if he groveled on his knees and apologized for every nasty thing he said about me and took them all back...I might consider it.

Maybe.

"You're too nice, Tina. Where did I go wrong? Sometimes it's like we don't even share the same DNA."

I wince and flick on my turn signal. Someone else finds me lacking and this time it's my own sister. "We have the same blonde hair and green eyes. Well, we do when you don't die your hair. What color is it this week?"

"Purple." Her sigh lasts several seconds. "Look, you need to stop pining over Jack. You're better off without him. I never liked him anyway."

"Are there any men you like? Besides Dad and Carter?"

"Men have their uses. Short term. Dad and Carter are the only ones I can tolerate on a regular basis."

"You might want to consider why our father and brother are the only men you tolerate."

"Don't try and change the subject on me. We're talking about you this morning."

The road to the school comes into view. Granite Cove Elementary shimmers in gold lettering on the hunter green wooden oval. They must have repainted the sign over the summer. I've been prepping my classroom for the start of the school year for almost a month, but this is the first time I noticed. Granted, I've been a tad preoccupied lamenting over the breakup.

My chest tightens and I get that combination of nerves and anticipation fluttering through my system. I love my work. Helping all those bright little minds discover something new—what's not to love?

Jack accused me of having no ambition—working and living in the same town I grew up in. Is he right? Am I just following along the easy path?

After graduating college, I never hesitated when the school offered me the position in Granite Cove. It didn't even occur to me to consider other towns in New Hampshire. I certainly didn't think about teaching in another state.

The sprawling brick building looms ahead. I've always gotten warm feelings looking at the familiar building before. Each addition provokes a fond memory from when I attended school here or a story from when my parents went here. We planted the various trees peppering the parking lot or grounds on past Arbor Days. Flowers fill the garden beds from past science experiments teaching the kids about plant life cycles. Have I trapped myself in a pretty prison based on happy memories?

"Did you lose your signal?"

I wince. How could I forget Jen is on the phone? "I'm in the school parking lot. I have to go. Talk later?"

"Okay, have a great first day. Forget about Jack. You know what you need? You need a rebound guy."

I drive around the side of the building to the teacher's lot and park. "A rebound guy?"

"Yeah, the dude you date once or twice after a breakup. He's not boyfriend material. He's the scorching hot make you drool a little bit guy who reminds you you're a sexy passionate woman. You need to find one of those."

"Right, I'll keep that in mind while I'm navigating the first day of school. I'm sure they'll be a ton of hot guys milling around the elementary school."

"You never know. One of your first graders might have a sexy dad, or there might be a new, male, teacher at the school. If you'd agree to go club hopping with me and my friends one night, I'm sure I could find one for you. How about Friday?"

I rest my forehead on the top of my steering wheel. Club hopping has never been my idea of a fun time. Should I give it a try? If nothing else, it will make Jen stop asking. I could take selfies of me and other guys and post them. How will Jack react if he sees the pictures on social media? Will he be jealous?

"Maybe. The first week of school is always crazy. I'll let you know later in the week."

"Fine, it's better than a no. Good luck. Love you."

"Love you." I hit the disconnect button on my steering wheel.

The buses will arrive soon. I need to get to my classroom and unload all my stuff and get back outside and greet my new students. I grab my giant woven tote bag, my purse, and the shopping bag full of rewards for the student treasure box which I forgot to buy last week while setting up my classroom.

Why did I linger over breakfast this morning? Oh yeah, it's the most important meal of the day and I wanted to treat myself to pancakes. Of course, the real time suck might have been checking my social media. And then, of course, I had to peek at Jack's pages only to discover he's having a blast out in California without me and making tons of new friends. At least according to his selfies, he is. Most of those new friends are women.

I might have liked to move across the country and start fresh. But he didn't ask me to go along—never even told me he applied for the position.

Hoisting my purse over my shoulder, I bump the car door closed with my hip. The tote and bag knock against my car and my purse strap slips off my shoulder.

I speed walk across the parking lot to the side entrance while trying to keep my purse from dragging on the ground by lifting my bags high enough in the air. My arms wobble under the strain. The glass doors are closing ahead of me behind another teacher. If I don't catch them, I'll have to put everything down and root around for my badge—which I should have remembered to take out ahead of time.

"Hold the door, please!"

A manicured hand with hot pink nails and gold rings holds open the door. I juggle my bags and plaster a smile on my face for my savior.

"Thanks so much!"

A tall lithe form steps into the open doorway. *Oh crud!* Not Lisette. Why couldn't it be anyone else but her?

She examines me from head to toe with no facial expression whatsoever. She doesn't smile or frown, not even a twitch from her pink lips. She's like a robot—a gorgeous, emotionless, perfect one who constantly makes me feel like an inept, frumpy, little, munchkin beside her. She personifies a Lisette, not a Lisa—which one of the other teachers joked her real name probably was. Maybe if my parents named me something more exotic than Tina, I wouldn't be boring old me.

"Lose your badge again?"

"No, it's in my bag." I only lost it a couple of times last year. It's not as if I lost it every month.

She looks at my bags and then at my dress. Her face doesn't move, but the disdain oozes out of her. I use my shoulder to push open the door and sidle in as she steps back.

"Your buttons don't line up."

I glance down. *Dang it!* My floral dress is scrunched over my chest because I skipped a buttonhole.

"Thanks." I give her a tight smile. She could have let me continue on without mentioning it, so maybe she's not so terrible after all.

"You know, there are affordable stylists. They're not only for the wealthy. I could ask mine if she knows one who could help someone like you."

And there's the dig.

She's wearing a form fitting black skirt and a white blouse. There's an assortment of gold necklaces filling her decolletage. Her long brown hair is straight and glossy. She's probably never had a bad hair day in her life.

"Gee thanks Lisette, but clothes have never been high in my priorities."

"Perhaps they should be." She glances over her shoulder. "The buses are arriving. You should set your alarm earlier, so you're not always late." She turns away and saunters down the hallway towards the front doors.

I jog in the opposite direction towards my classroom with my bags banging against my legs. I'm not always late.

Fine, I am, but I'm working on it.

Monica steps out of the adjoining hallway linking the higher grades with the preschool, kindergarten, and first-grade classrooms. "Hey, no running in the hall, Miss Cooper." She chuckles. "Need help?"

"No, got it, thanks." I halt in front of my door. On second thought…I frown and glance back over my shoulder.

"Here." Monica reaches past me and opens the door.

"You're a lifesaver, thanks." I dump all my bags in my chair behind my desk and stride back to the door.

Monica frowns and points to my dress. "I think…"

"Oh right, I forgot." I fix my buttons as we traipse down the hallway. Hopefully, I won't flash anyone in the process.

Her gray blouse and black pants are classy and professional. The pearl earrings and necklace are a nice touch too. Is Lisette right? Should I put more effort into my appearance?

"You want to grab a coffee after school today and celebrate making it through the first day of school unscathed?"

I chuckle and smile. "Can't today. I promised my mom I would help her plant the slew of shrubs she came home with over the weekend. There was a sale and my mom cannot pass up a sale. Raincheck?"

Monica laughs. "Absolutely."

The morning shuffle of getting the students to the right rooms goes off without too many mishaps. My kids hang up their shiny new backpacks on the hooks with their names over them and find their desks.

Sniffles and hiccups of distress come from the open door. A man carrying a little girl wearing a pink dress and white leggings stands there. A small pink backpack is looped over his shoulder. Her blonde head is buried in his neck, but the familiar nametags with the rainbow in the corner and my name and room number tells me she's in the right place. She must be the missing Hope Swanson from the quick attendance check I skimmed over a few minutes ago. A new student, not only to my first-grade class, but to Granite Cove. They added her to my class list last month.

I put a wide smile on my face and walk over to the door.

"Hi there. You must be Hope. I'm Miss Cooper and I'm so excited you're in my class this year."

Two sets of identical milk chocolate brown eyes with specs of gold stare at me. One behind a pair of silver wire-rimmed glasses and the other peeks at me from, I'm guessing, her father's shoulder. She sniffles.

"Nice to meet you. I'm Ron Swanson. Hope, say hello to your teacher." He squats and tries to put her down, but she's having none of it and keeps her arms and legs wrapped around him.

His warm voice reminds me of thick, dark, molasses and a flutter stirs in my belly.

I inhale a shaky breath and bend over so I'm eye level with Hope. She needs to be my focus, not her handsome father—which I have no business noticing how handsome he is.

"I know it can be a little scary the first day in a new school, but I promise I'm pretty nice and not scary at all. Do you like cats?"

Hope peeks at me with one eye and nods once.

"It just so happens that our class mascot is my cat, Snickers. Now, I obviously can't bring my actual cat to school every day, but I have a stuffed cat that looks just like him. See that brown tabby cat on my desk?"

Another careful nod.

"Each day, the student with the most stars for good behavior gets to have Snickers sit on their desk the next day. Since this is the first day of school, no one has earned any stars yet. Would you like to be the very first one to have Snickers on their desk this year?"

She lifts her head, bites her lip, and nods.

"Great! Why don't you say goodbye to your dad?" I glance at the man and lift my eyebrow in question. He nods. "I'll show you where to hang up your backpack, and then we'll get Snickers and find your desk."

I hold out my hand to her with a smile. She places her small hand in mine and glances around the classroom for the first time.

She looks up at her dad and squeezes my hand tight.

He kisses her on top of her head and hands her the backpack. "You'll have a wonderful time and I'll be here to pick you up at the end of the day, okay?"

She nods and whispers, "promise?"

"I promise."

"Okay."

"Let's go find your name plate over your hook. Do you think you can spot your name before I can?"

I tug her hand towards the hooks lined up to the right of the door.

She points to her name and shuffles over.

"You found it fast. Excellent job. Hang up your backpack."

There's a deep sigh behind me. I glance over my shoulder at the door while Hope hangs up her backpack.

Her father nods and mouths the word *thank you* before turning and leaving.

That little flutter dances around inside me again.

Nope, one of my students' dads is definitely not a man I should notice and certainly not a candidate for the rebound guy Jen advocated for.

Chapter Two

Hope's father is late for the conference. My last set of parents left ten minutes ago. The school doesn't allow much time for each meeting. If he doesn't show up soon, I'll have to cancel because the next fifteen minute slot is full.

I really want to discuss Hope's progress with him. She's still shy and hesitant to participate in class, but she's so smart and helpful to all the students.

I should just peek down the hallway and see if he's out there. I use the round table as leverage and scoot back the chair. Because of these kid sized chairs, I'm thankful every day for my five-foot two-inch frame. It's almost painful watching the taller parents lower and rise from these chairs.

Multiple voices and soft laughter drift down the hallway. All feminine sounding so not Hope's Dad. I stick the top of my head out and peer up and down the corridor.

A group of women, including Lisette, are in a circle halfway down the hallway. She's not one to overtly socialize with parents or teachers. She usually stands off to the side, watching.

Lisette shifts and props her fist on her hip. Ah, now it's clear why she and the other women are there. Hope's dad is in the middle of them.

It's been that way every morning and afternoon when he drops off and picks up Hope.

The single and not so single women congregate around him. A small hand tugs on his shirt. Hope must be with him. He adjusts his glasses and lifts his head. When his gaze meets mine, he lifts a hand and sidles past Lisette and the other women with an absent smile. He murmurs something to them, but he's too far away for me to hear. Hope's hand is clasped in his. She waves and breaks into a jog, matching his long stride.

I pop my head back into my classroom, smooth my hair, and check my buttons are all lined up and fastened. I shake my head and dash back to the table. I will not be one of those women fawning over the rare, single, handsome dad around here. It's like he's a unicorn or something and women are in a frenzy.

He strides in with a smile. "Sorry I'm late."

Hope rushes over and gives me a hug. She's such a sweetheart.

I glance at the clock. Half the meeting time has passed. "Please have a seat, Mr. Swanson. Hope, do you want to go play on the rug while I talk to your dad?"

Hope nods and walks over to the toy bins lined up alongside the colorful rug depicting the solar system.

His gaze tracks her until she chooses a puzzle and settles on the rug.

"Sorry, I've yet to find a babysitter."

"That's okay. You're not the only parent to bring their kids with them."

I shift through my papers and slide Hope's Halloween painting of a witch and a cat towards him. "Hope is quite an artist."

He grins as he picks up the paper. "She gets that from her mother. I have enough trouble drawing stick figures."

I nibble on my bottom lip. I've heard the gossip circulating the school. He's a widower. If the rumors are true, his wife died in a car accident a couple of years ago. Poor Hope. How awful it must be losing your mother so young.

"Your wife was an artist?"

"Not professionally, but she painted as a hobby. She talked about pursuing it someday during one of those *what if* conversations. You know when you tell each other what you'd do if money or responsibilities weren't factors?"

He stares at Hope with a sad smile. Missing his wife? Does Hope resemble her? His hair is light brown, not blonde like Hope's. They have the same eyes, though. His yellow shirt complements the gold flecks in his eyes and his tan skin.

I pull her assessment sheet in front of me. "Hope is doing very well academically. She meets or surpasses all her benchmarks."

"I'll take credit for that one," he says with a chuckle. "Everything else positive is probably from Ruth, but school smarts, I'll claim."

I smile and hand him a copy. "Did well in school?"

He shrugs. "Well enough. I'm an accountant, so math is my strongest subject."

"Hope gets along well with others. She participates in small group settings, but she rarely raises her hand during class. If I call on her directly, she usually whispers the answer or ducks her head. There's nothing wrong with that. We all have unique personalities. I just wanted to make you aware and tell you it's my belief that it stems from shyness rather than not understanding the work or a refusal to answer."

"She never used to be shy. Before the accident...before she lost her mother, she was the chattiest little kid to everyone. Never met a stranger. It used to worry me a little. You know, not having any stranger danger?"

He rubs the back of his neck. "After Ruth died, Hope withdrew. She changed. I thought it was part of grieving and she would come out of it. She has a bit. At her last school, they talked about her not being ready for kindergarten because she missed so many days of preschool. She was inconsolable and refused to go to school. What was I to do? Force her after she just lost her mother?"

"I don't see any developmental delays or any reason she's not ready for first-grade."

"Thank you. I believe a lot of that has to do with you. You're one of her favorite people. Every afternoon when she gets in the car, she talks about what Miss Cooper said or did."

"That's certainly nice to hear. She's a joy to have in class."

"It makes moving to Granite Cove seem like the right decision.

Moving away from family and friends was hard, but I think it's been good for Hope. Now if I could just find a babysitter..."

Mom might be interested. She occasionally watches the neighbors' kids. She mentioned doing something part-time.

"My mother is a retired preschool teacher and lives here in town. I don't know if it would work for either of you, but I could mention it to her if you like."

"That would be fantastic." He withdraws a business card from his wallet and writes a phone number on the back. "Here's my number. Please have her call me if she's interested."

"I will."

I spot the twins' mother through the window in the door and peek at the clock. It's time for my next meeting. "Do you have any questions for me?"

"No, I don't think so. My mind is still fixated on the possibility of finding a babysitter."

I smile and gather Hope's papers together. "Like I said, I can't make any promises, but I'll talk to her. If you do think of any questions, you can always call or email me." I stand and hold out my hand.

"Thank you." His hand engulfs mine. He smiles down at me and heat washes over me.

Please don't let me be blushing!

I pull my hand away and turn towards Hope, who has already put everything away and is skipping over to us. "Good job cleaning up. I'll see you tomorrow, Hope."

She grins and gives me a hug. "Bye Miss Cooper."

I trail behind them as they walk out the door. Olivia pushes away from the wall and smiles at them both. "Hi Hope. Is this your dad?"

Hope nods and gives her a shy smile.

"I'm Timmy and Tommy's mom." Olivia holds out her hand to Mr. Swanson and he shakes it briefly.

"Nice to meet you. The twins, right? Hope has mentioned you're in the class helping with the spelling words."

"That's me. Hope is an excellent speller."

Hope ducks her head against her father's leg while he nods and says, "thank you."

Olivia turns to me. "Are you ready to tell me how my little monsters are doing?"

I laugh and wave her inside. They're a bit rambunctious, but they're good kids. They're always on their best behavior on the days their mom is here to help out. Lucky for me, she volunteered to be the room parent, so she's here often.

She shuts the door and then fans her hand in front of her face. "Now I see what all the fuss is about. Hope's dad is a hotty."

Chapter Three

"Hey there! I'm so glad I ran into you. I'm planning the first book club meeting. Are you still interested?"

I blink at Monica, grinning above my table. *Book club?*

"Remember we talked about it over coffee a few weeks ago?"

"Oh, right, sorry, I forgot for a second."

She'd suggested forming a book club with a couple of other teachers. It sounded fun. I do need to socialize outside my family more. Currently, my social calendar has only family dinners and obligations listed. All my high school and college friends drifted away after I started dating Jack. He would sulk when I went out with friends, so I stopped. Now I have neither my friends, nor Jack.

Monica places her hands on the top of the chair opposite me.

"Do you want to sit?"

"Thanks, but I can't. I'm picking up a pizza for my brother and me."

Maybe she needs to hang out with people she's not related to too.

"When's the first meeting, and what's the book?"

She grins. "The week after Halloween at my house. We'll have time to recoup after all the school parties and a minute to breathe before preparing for Thanksgiving. I chose a paranormal romance about witches."

"Sounds appropriate for the holiday."

"That's what I thought too. I'll text you the book and party details, okay?"

I nod. "Thanks, I'm looking forward to it. Who else will be there?"

"So far, we've only a got a handful. Kerry Barton, a teacher from the high school. My Aunt Aggie, who is technically my godmother, but I've always called her my aunt. Sally Smith, a former teacher, as you know, and you. Feel free to bring along anyone you'd like."

Kerry is nice. I only met her a few times, but she was always friendly. I suppose I could ask my mom to come, but then that would sort of defeat the purpose of spending time with people I'm not related to.

"What should I bring?"

"Just yourself. We'll figure out all the logistics of future meetings that night with everyone there."

The hostess behind the counter calls out, "Frasier?"

Monica turns her head and her brown hair swings against her cheek. She raises her hand. "That's me."

I chuckle. I tend to raise my hand too. School habits are hard to break, especially when you teach them to your students every day.

"I'll talk to you later. I'm so excited we're finally getting the book club going."

"Me too."

I glance back down at my plastic menu. Joe's Pizzeria is the best place to get pizza in town. I had a craving, but now looking around at all the full tables, I wish I'd ordered to go too. It's lonely eating by myself and even though no one is openly staring in my direction, I can't help feeling like they're whispering about poor, dumb, Tina who got dumped instead of proposed to.

It's my own fault. If I hadn't been so excited and sure Jack was going to propose, I wouldn't have talked about it to everyone I knew. Then the whispers and looks would only be about him dumping me and not the added bonus of me expecting a proposal and a ring.

A cool breeze blows against my bare ankles and flutters the hem of my skirt against my calves. The open door of the restaurant fills with a familiar, tall, figure and his constant companion. Hope's gaze lands on me and she waves enthusiastically.

"Miss Cooper! Miss Cooper!" Hope pulls her hand free from her father's, runs to my table, and throws her little arms around me.

Is there anything better than the affection of a child?

It's pure and unentangled with adult emotions like judgment or pity.

There's still a hint of scent from the strawberry shampoo in her hair. She had me sniff it this morning in class after whispering in my ear about the new shampoo her daddy bought her at the store.

"Did you burn your dinner, too? Daddy burned the chicken, and the kitchen filled with smoke when he opened the oven. The smoke alarm was really loud, and I covered my ears. Don't tell Daddy, but I'd rather have pizza than chicken."

"Busted, I heard that."

Hope's father rests his hands on top of the chair the same way Monica did and winks.

Was that aimed at me or Hope? It had to be her, of course.

Though his gaze *had* flickered over me when he did it.

Hope giggles and leans her head against my arm.

I smile at her and glance up at her father. "Cooking isn't one of my favorite activities, either. I've set the smoke alarm off myself once or twice."

Okay, it's been more than that. Jack used to joke every time I invited him over for dinner about whether or not I would forget and burn the meal.

"I like to say my cooking skills are a work in progress." He chuckles as his gaze rests on my face.

A giddy warmth fills my body, and I resist the desire to fan my cheeks.

Boy, does he have some sort of attraction superpower? I get that he's a handsome single dad and all, but it's not like he's celebrity gorgeous or anything. Why does he make me feel like a blushing teenager every time he comes around?

There is something about his smile. And his hair. He's got thick hair and the brown locks have a tint of red when the sun hits them just right. Then there are those eyes. The thin silver rims of his glasses only highlight rather than hide the amazing color. They're this golden brown like a lion.

One of his brown eyebrows lifts. *Lord, I've been staring and fantasizing about him like an idiot.* I clear my throat.

"I'll have to borrow that line the next time someone makes a joke about my cooking." I smooth my eggplant-colored skirt over my legs. It's hopelessly wrinkled, just like my ivory top. His white button down and dark gray pants are smooth as glass. Does he iron his own clothes or send them out? Every time I iron, I swear my clothes end up looking worse than when I started.

"Watching cooking shows is my new hobby." He glances down at Hope. "One of us has to learn and, unfortunately, Hope has a valid excuse being only six."

I smirk. "There is that."

"Are you getting pizza too, Miss Cooper?"

I smile at Hope. "Yes, I am. I had a craving."

"My favorite is cheese. I don't like stuff all over it."

"I like cheese too, but sometimes I like to try some toppings. It's always fun to try new things, isn't it? Otherwise, how will we discover what we like?"

Hope wrinkles her forehead and considers my words.

She holds up a finger. "I'll try one, but only one 'cause I might not like it mixed with something else. And on only part of the pizza 'cause if I don't like it, then I'll want my cheese."

"That sounds like a good plan."

I peek up at her father hoping I haven't overstepped. Sometimes I forget to stop teaching outside the classroom.

Both his eyebrows are raised and he's smiling. I guess it's a pleasant surprise Hope is trying something new.

"Daddy, is it okay if we share a pizza with Miss Cooper?"

"Oh, Hope, I don't want to intrude on your dinner."

"I think it's us that are intruding on yours." He glances around the restaurant. "Hope, we should let Miss Cooper enjoy her dinner and find ourselves a table."

"But she's all alone. Why can't we sit right here?"

"Perhaps she's expecting someone to join her."

Hope frowns and studies me. "Are you?"

My cheeks heat and I shake my head. "No." How do I give him an out without upsetting Hope? Surely the last thing he wants to do is have dinner with his daughter's teacher.

"Well, if you don't mind...?" His hand grips the chair closest to Hope.

"Of course not, you're more than welcome."

Hope claps her hands and hops into the chair he pulls out for her. "Now we can share a pizza!"

I laugh as he takes the chair across from me.

The waitress stops at the table with an absentminded smile. "Ready to order?"

"Oh." I hand him my menu. "I don't think they've had a chance to decide."

"I think we're going with a pizza. Half cheese and half..." He glances at me. "Can I convince you to get sausage?"

"You can."

He hands the menu to the waitress. "We'll have a cola, apple juice, and..." He looks back to me.

"Ginger ale for me please."

With a half nod, the waitress heads toward the kitchen.

"Do I like sausage, Daddy?"

"You do with breakfast sometimes."

"Okay."

The waitress returns and plops down additional utensils wrapped in a white napkin before walking away.

"Joe's Pizzeria has the best pizza around. Trust me, I've lived here my whole life and tried all of them."

Hope's eyes grow wide. "Your whole life?"

"Yup, well, I lived in a dorm during college but I was here for summers and holidays." *And most weekends too.*

"How long have you been a teacher?"

I glance from Hope to her father. "Three years."

"Was teaching the career you always wanted?"

"For as long as I can remember...well, there was a brief period where I wished to be a doctor. That changed rather quickly once I passed out at the sight of blood when my brother fell off his bike and scraped his knee.”

He chuckles. “Not a fan of blood?”

“No, thankfully I haven’t passed out in quite some time, but it still makes me queasy. What about you? Have you always wanted to be an accountant?”

“Definitely not. Let’s see, first it was a professional baseball player. Then it was soccer and back to baseball. A few months of guitar lessons made me think I would be a rock star. Then around my junior or senior year of high school, I began to think those might not be the most realistic aspirations since I was terrible at all three.”

I laugh and cover my mouth with my hand.

The waitress delivers our drinks. I murmur, “thank you,” and receive a small smile before she’s called to another table. Joe’s is usually busy, especially on a Friday night, but it seems everyone had the same idea to have dinner out tonight. All the tables are now full and there’s a line at the takeout counter.

“I met Ruth, Hope’s mom, and decided business might be a better choice. Once I got to college, I sort of fell into accounting. I discovered I have a knack for numbers and details.”

“High school sweethearts?”

He nods and smiles.

“What’s that mean, Daddy?”

“It means your mother and I met, and started dating when we were in high school.”

I sip my soda. It was sad enough before thinking about Hope and her father losing her mother, but how heartbreaking it must be to lose the person you basically grew up loving. I started dating Jack my senior year in college and it felt like a lost a limb when he left.

But he didn’t die—he dumped me. And moved on like I never existed. I guess I was a lot more invested than he was. So why am I still thinking about him?

“Oh, then you had me.”

He chuckles. “Well, first we went to college, got married, got jobs, then had you.” He looks sideways at me. “I’m significantly older than your Miss Cooper.”

How old does he think I am? I'm not a kid. "I'm twenty-five."

"And I'm thirty-five."

Ten years. I wouldn't have guessed, but still that's not an enormous difference.

"Where are you from?"

"Cape Cod."

"Not too far from Granite Cove."

"A few hours. Hope's grandparents think we moved to another planet."

Hope nods. "They miss me a lot."

"I bet they do."

"Grammy and Grandpa came to see our new house and I'm going to visit Nanna and Pops next month."

"That's nice. I'm sure you must miss them too."

She nods and rocks her feet back and forth while she sips her juice.

"We needed a fresh start and my company made me an offer I couldn't refuse."

"Granite Cove is lucky to have you both."

"It's been an adjustment, but I think we're both finding our groove."

The pizza arrives steaming and smelling delicious. I unwrap the napkin from my utensils and place it in my lap. Hope watches me closely and does the same.

"Did my mother get in touch with you? I gave her your card and told her how you're looking for a sitter."

Mom lit up like the fourth of July. I'm not sure if it was the prospect of babysitting or of a single dad for one of her single daughters. She quizzed me on everything I knew about Hope and her dad. I made her promise no matchmaking. Mom grew silent, but then reluctantly promised.

"She did and I'm forever in your debt. She starts next week." He slides a piece of sausage pizza to his plate, cuts it in half, and then puts a piece on Hope's plate.

"Oh good. I'm so glad it worked out."

Hope frowns at the pizza. "She seems nice. Not as nice as you, though."

"I promise she's just as nice." I place a slice of pizza on my plate and smile at her. "After all, she raised me. And do you know what?"

"What?"

"My parents have a big, goofy, dog named Moose. And…if you're going to be at her house then you're likely to see me from time to time too since I live over the garage."

"Really?"

I nod.

Her face lights up in a wide smile.

"That's a bonus." Her father takes another piece of pizza.

I thought I'd be moving out and finding a place with Jack once we married, but it looks like the apartment over the garage is my home for the foreseeable future. I can't afford any place else unless I get roommates. A bunch of them.

Hope picks up her skinny slice and nibbles at the end. She touches the tip of her tongue to one of two balls of sausage on the pizza and scrunches her face together. "I don't think I like it."

"Take one bite and if you don't like it, then you can have the cheese." He points to her plate and raises one finger.

She twists her mouth from side to side. "Okay, one."

Hope sighs heavily and takes a delicate bite. She chews and shakes her head.

"Not for you, huh? Well, I'm glad you tried it. Good job." He takes the rest of the slice off her plate and gives her a plain cheese one.

"I'm proud of you, Hope. Now you can cross one of the possible pizza toppings off your list." I take a second piece for myself.

"How many more are there?"

"I'm not sure, but we can look at a menu and count them."

"We'll have to come back and try each one, right Miss Cooper?" Hope stares at me with the pizza in her hands.

"I guess so."

"There might even be a few on the menu that Miss Cooper hasn't tried. She'll have to see if she likes them. I doubt there's any I haven't tried, however. I am a pizza aficionado."

"What's a fish…a fish do?"

He chuckles and taps Hope on the end of her nose. "Aficionado. It means I really like pizza and have eaten a lot of it."

"Oh, I want to be one too."

"Well then it's settled the three of us will have to return and try every pizza on the menu."

Hope claps and then takes an exaggerated chomp out of her pizza.

Wait, he wants us to come back together? As in future pizza dates? Is he interested in me romantically?

No, he must mean as a friend. He pointed out how young he thinks I am, so it's doubtful he's attracted to me.

"Are we in agreement, Miss Cooper? Are you up for a pizza challenge?" He takes a bite of his pizza and points it at me. "Or are you chicken?"

"I am not chicken, Mr. Swanson, and have in fact eaten chicken on pizza. And there may be a few things I haven't tried on the menu, but I consider myself a pizza aficionado as well and feel quite up to the challenge."

"Then I think it's time you called me Ron. What's your stance on anchovies?"

My lips twitch. "I don't think they belong on a pizza. How do you feel about pineapple?"

"As long as it's accompanied by ham, I'm rather amenable. Taco pizza?"

"I'm a fan. Clams?"

"Seafood and pizza should not be eaten together."

"I concur."

He grins. "Now here's the big test. Vegetables."

Hope's head swivels back and forth between her father and me.

"Besides the aforementioned lettuce and tomato on the taco pizza, I would have to say that vegetables do not belong on a pizza." I peek at Hope's wide-eyed face. "They are, however, a necessary and delicious food group."

"We're a perfect pizza match."

That's definitely flirting—isn't it?

Chapter Four

Mom glances over her shoulder when the doorbell sounds.

"Will you get that? Your sister and brother wouldn't knock, so it must be Ron and Hope."

"Sure." I set the last biscuit on the baking sheet and wash my hands in the sink.

Mom invited them to Christmas dinner after hearing they would spend the holiday alone. Hope literally bounced up and down when she told me last week in class. According to Mom, Ron's parents are on a cruise and Hope's other grandparents are visiting their new grandchild which Ruth's sister just gave birth to.

I've only seen Ron from a waving distance since we shared a pizza. He hasn't invited me for another ingredient taste test challenge like he joked about. It must have been just that, a joke. So much for my flirting theory. He must be one of those guys that naturally flirts with everyone.

Hope has her little nose pressed against the narrow window next to the front door. Her hands frame her face and she's peering inside. A grin stretches across her face when she spots me walking down the hall.

When I open the door, she launches herself at my waist and squeezes. "Hi Miss Cooper!"

I hug her back and laugh. "Merry Christmas, Hope."

"Merry Christmas! It's snowing out. Did you see?"

I glance out over the front porch as I step back to let her and her father step inside. There are big, fat snowflakes drifting down. A foot of snow already coats the ground from previous storms.

"Looks like we have a white Christmas." I smile at Ron as he passes me carrying a bottle of wine, a box of candy, and a bouquet of flowers.

"I wasn't sure what your mother prefers. She insisted I not bring anything, but my mother taught me to never show up empty handed."

I chuckle. "She'll be thrilled with any of the three."

"Look, look, look!" Hope jumps up and down and points above our heads.

A kissing ball of mistletoe dangles above with a red bow. When did that get there? I arrived through the back door like I always do, but since when does my mother hang a kissing ball for Christmas?

"Well, we must follow the rules of the house." Ron leans down and his lips brush mine.

Hope claps her hands and giggles.

I firm my wobbly smile. My cheeks heat as he stares. I turn away and bend down to Hope. "It's only fair you get a kiss too." I kiss her chilly cheek. "Let me help you with your coat and boots."

After I help her, she skips down the hallway to the kitchen. Ron puts his packages down on the bench and hangs his coat up on the hooks. Should I say I've never seen the kissing ball before? I certainly don't want him thinking I planned it.

I bet my mother did, however. The question is for me or my sister? I got her promise not to match make with Ron and I, but she didn't include Jen in the promise.

Is Ron Jen's type? Does she even have a type? Is she Ron's? He did say his wife was an artist. Jen is an artist.

"Hello there."

My dad stands in the archway to the living room. Ron walks over and shakes his hand.

"Merry Christmas, Frank. Thanks for inviting us."

"You and that little girl of yours are always welcome. Speaking of, where is Hope?"

I point down the hall. "I hear her chattering with Mom in the kitchen."

Ron picks up his gifts. "I wasn't sure what you or Jane liked so I brought an assortment."

Dad chuckles. "I'm partial to the chocolates myself, but I know Jane will appreciate the pretty flowers. I'm sure we'll all enjoy a glass of the wine with dinner."

He's on a first name basis with my parents. Not surprising, Mom has been babysitting Hope for almost two months and they've never been overly formal people. I follow Dad and Ron down the hall as they chitchat about the Patriots winning last Sunday's game. My father must be thrilled he found someone else he can talk about football with.

In the kitchen, Hope stands on a step stool next to Mom wrapping dough over a round of brie. I walk around to the other side of the island they're working on. "What an excellent job you're doing, Hope. That's one of my favorite appetizers."

Mom pats her on the shoulder before walking over and greeting Ron.

"There are red berries on the bottom." Hope tilts her head as she peers at the appetizer.

"Cranberries. When it comes out of the oven, the cheese is melted and warm." I rub my hand over my belly. "It's so good."

"Merry Christmas!" Carter bellows from the front door.

Hope's eyes widen and she stares down the hall.

"That's my brother, Carter. My sister, Jennifer should be here soon too."

"Already am." Jen walks into the kitchen and snags a shrimp from the bowl. Her hair is bright red and super short except for the top where it stands straight up. The black turtleneck sweater and red plaid leggings are both form fitting. My beautiful sister has never had trouble attracting men.

"Hey Sis." She bumps my shoulder and leans on the island with her elbows on the counter and her jaw in her hands. "Hey kiddo. You must be the Hope I've been hearing so much about."

Hope nods silently.

"There's a rumor you might have taken the role of Candyland champion from me. You'll have to beat me first. Challenge accepted?"

Hope smiles and nods.

Jen holds out her hand for a fist bump and Hope giggles as she bumps her little fist against Jen's.

"Now hold on a minute, Hope has to beat all of us if she wants to be crowned the Cooper Candyland champion." Carter puts his arms across Jen and my shoulders. "Do you think you have what it takes to beat all three of us?"

Hope places her hand over her mouth as she laughs. Ron walks over and kisses the top of her head.

Carter stretches a hand across the island. "I'm Carter. Nice to meet you."

Ron shakes his hand and then holds his hand out to Jen.

I hold my breath. When I introduced Jack to her and he offered his hand, she looked him up and down and walked away as she told him if he hurt her little sister, she'd make him wish he'd never been born.

Maybe that's why he moved across the country when he dumped me.

Jen shakes his hand. "Merry Christmas."

She must like Ron. Of course, I'm not dating him either.

"Is your hair red because it's Christmas?" Hope frowns as she studies Jen's hair.

I purse my lips together.

Ron puts his hand on Hope's shoulder. "Hope..."

Jen leans on the counter. "Sure is. I thought about adding a green stripe to either side but didn't get around to it. What do you think?"

Hope tilts her head from side to side while she stares at Jen's hair. "Can you do a green Christmas tree?"

"Hmm...now you're talking kid. I could have the shape of a tree shaved into the sides."

"Instead of hairstyles, why don't we start on the appetizers?" Mom waves a hand towards the array of food set up on the end of the island in Christmas themed dishes and puts the stuffed brie into the oven.

We all shift down and delve into the crackers, sweet and sour meatballs, and veggies and dip. I eye the oven waiting for the brie while I nibble on a carrot and then a meatball.

"Mom, is this a new recipe?" I stare at the half-eaten meatball on the end of the toothpick in my hand.

She nods as she plucks a shrimp from the bowl. "I found a cranberry barbeque recipe. Do you like it?"

I stuff the rest of it into my mouth and chew while I nod. "It's fantastic."

"Have to agree with you there, pipsqueak." Carter leans in front of me to grab another meatball.

I hesitate before grabbing another one for myself, but then do an internal shrug and take one. I'll still have room for the brie. Probably not dinner, but there are always leftovers. Mom never fails to send us each home with a stack of leftovers. Overeating is like a rite of passage for the holidays anyway—sort of like Carter calling me pipsqueak. He's been doing it forever, and not likely to stop despite my vociferous protests when I was a teenager. I suppose being older and a foot taller than me imbues him with certain big brother allowances.

Ron appears beside me. "I better try these meatballs before they disappear."

I scan his dark green sweater and black pants. I've never seen him in a pair of jeans. He's always dressed more formally. I peek down at my cream-colored sweater with a bright green Christmas tree in the center and my green leggings. I was going for festive, but I should have worn something more hip like Jen. Even Mom is dressed more stylishly than me. Her red cashmere sweater and black jeans hug her trim frame and her black ankle boots give her a couple inches of added height.

Carter grabs a bowl and scoops a half dozen meatballs, at least, into a pile.

"Carter! Save some for the rest of us." Jen swats at his hand from across the island.

"Don't worry, there's plenty more still in the crock pot." Mom points to it on the stove before she opens the oven door and removes the sizzling brie.

I take a deep inhale of the sweet scent permeating the kitchen and peek over at Ron standing next to me. He's smiling at Jen and Carter bickering over the meatballs. His hair has grown. There's a slight curl at the ends now. Is he letting it grow out, or has he just not bothered to get a haircut? I like the more casual look on him. Although, I liked the precise haircut on him too.

Mom places the Christmas platter with the brie next to the plate of crackers. I grab the small Christmas tree shaped cheese knife and slice into the side of the pastry covered brie. White cheese oozes out mixed with dark red cranberries.

Mom chuckles. "Tina has insisted on being the first to partake of the brie since I started making it years ago."

Carter hands me a paper plate with a Santa Claus in the center. "She's territorial about it too, so watch out."

Ron laughs. I hand him the brie I sliced. "I know how to share." I give my brother the evil eye and slice another piece for myself.

"Wow. She must really like you."

My cheeks heat as I refuse to look at Ron, my brother, or anyone else in the kitchen. I pop the cracker with the brie into my mouth and chew.

Ron leans close and whispers, "you're right, this is delicious. I don't blame you for wanting to be the first."

Hope tugs on my sweater and pops her head between us. "I helped make it Daddy. Can I have a piece, Miss Cooper?"

"Of course you can." I slice a small piece for her and put it on a cracker. She sniffs it and peers at it from all sides before nibbling a piece. "It's sweet."

Ron smiles down at his daughter. "Do you like it?"

"I think so." She takes another small bite and then nods. "I do."

Mom and Dad laugh from the other side of the island.

"Keep eating everyone, but don't fill up. Save room for dinner." Mom walks over to the stove and stirs something in a pot.

"Let's zip you up. It's cold out there." I adjust Hope's pink coat and zip it while she peers down at my hands and then yawns.

"It's way past your bedtime." Ron hands her a pair of matching pink mittens.

There's a bag stuffed with leftovers from Christmas dinner sitting on the bench by the front door for them to take with them. Ron pulls on his black, wool, coat while Hope slides her hands into the mittens.

"Oh, I forgot my new doll!" Hope turns and runs back into the living room where Dad has dozed off.

"Your parents are so good to her."

"They love her. They get to experience a little of what being grandparents is like. I'm surprised the less than subtle questions about when me and my siblings are going to settle down and produce some haven't skyrocketed."

"Do you want kids?"

"Only about a half dozen or so."

He laughs. "That many, huh?"

I smile and shrug. "I've always wanted kids and I want them to have brothers and sisters to grow up with."

"Yeah, Hope agrees with you on that one. She asked for a baby brother or sister for Christmas."

"Did she?"

"I ended up telling her that Santa would need more time to work on such a big wish." He shrugs. "I'm not sure if that was the right thing to say or not, but I was at a loss and I didn't want to tell her no outright or get into any awkward conversations she's too young for."

"She might forget, or you might have just made her think that a little patience will grant her wish."

"That was my thought too." He points up. "Looks like we find ourselves here again."

I glance up at the kissing ball hanging over his head this time. He wants a kiss?

His eyebrows lift as if to say, "well?"

A smile twitches at my lips and I take a step closer. I lean up to place a chaste kiss on his cheek, but he turns his head and my lips land on his.

The breath stutters in my chest.

He applies a slight pressure as our lips linger together.

Running footsteps approach from the hall.

We pull apart when Hope appears with her doll.

"I forgot she was in the kitchen. Remember, Miss Cooper, she helped us wash dishes?"

"You're right, she did. Was my mother still in the kitchen?"

She said her goodbyes and then disappeared after mumbling something about calling my aunt.

"Uh huh, she helped me find her."

"Time to go, Hope. Say goodbye to Miss Cooper." He picks up the bag of leftovers.

Hope gives me a squeeze. "Bye Miss Cooper."

"Bye Hope. Merry Christmas."

Ron opens the door and Hope shuffles out. An ice-cold breeze rushes into the room and I wrap my arms around myself.

"Merry Christmas, Tina."

My gaze darts to him as he walks out. "Merry Christmas, Ron." I nibble my lip as the door shuts behind him.

That kiss meant something, right?

That was more than an obligatory mistletoe kiss.

"That was a lovely Christmas, wasn't it?"

I whirl around. Mom stands in the archway.

"Yes, it was really nice that you invited them."

She smiles and searches my face. For what exactly, I'm not sure. But I'm beginning to suspect that my mother had ulterior motives.

"How was your call with Aunt Holly?"

"Hmm?"

"You said you had to call her, remember?"

"Oh, yes. I wanted to tell her about the meatball recipe."

"What did she say?"

She waves a hand. "Oh, I left a message. I'll talk to her tomorrow."

I narrow my eyes and fold my arms over my stomach.

Mom and my aunt are more than sisters. They've been best friends and confidants since the cradle. They're only a year apart and they always pick up if one of them calls the other. The conversations can easily last an hour.

"You promised not to match make, Mom."

A little smirk appears at the corner of her mouth. "Something tells me I won't have to."

Chapter Five

The tips of my fingers are numb. I should know better than to not wear gloves in the middle of January. I do know better, but I'm running late for my dentist appointment and I prefer not to waste time searching for them. I could have sworn I left them in my purse or my coat pocket, but they weren't in either. I should get one of those locator thingies that you put on items you lose all the time.

"Need some help?"

I startle and the ice scraper slips from my frozen fingers and bounces off my windshield to the slush covered parking lot.

Ron bends over and scoops it up. He's bundled up in a navy coat and thick black gloves. A chill shivers through me. I'm not sure if it's from the cold or the memory of our Christmas kiss. I've fixated on the moment too many times in the two weeks since it happened. I paced my apartment every time I knew he'd be picking up or dropping off Hope at my mom's. I half hoped he would knock on my door or call. The other half of me knew I was reading too much into the innocent kiss.

He's my student's father, it would be unethical for me to date him even if he got around to asking.

He glances at my hands as he scrapes the fresh snow off my windshield. "Where are your gloves?"

I shrug and stuff my hands in my coat pockets. "I seem to have misplaced them. You don't have to do that."

"What sort of gentleman would I be if I let my daughter's teacher catch hypothermia clearing off her car with no gloves on?"

Daughter's teacher? Yup, that's all I am.

"Where is Hope?" I scan the school parking lot. All the busses and parents that pick their kids up in the afternoon have left.

"She's on her first official playdate since we moved. I swung by to make sure she didn't change her mind at the last minute and for my own peace of mind."

"That's great. She's really opening up in class and making friends."

"Yeah, it helps make me think I made the right decision moving here."

"Have you been questioning it?"

He shrugs and drops the windshield wiper back into place. "As a single parent, I question most of my decisions."

"You're doing a wonderful job. Anyone can see that."

He smiles and dusts the snow off his gloves. "Thanks."

"Thank you for clearing off the snow for me."

"You'd already done most of it." He taps the toe of his boot against my tire. "Looks a little worn. You should probably see about a replacement."

Dad mentioned the same thing before the school break. I meant to take care of it then.

"Snow tires might be a good idea too. With a couple of feet of snow already on the ground and more predicted, these tires aren't safe."

"I'm not helpless. I've lived here all my life. I know how to drive in the snow and how to maintain my car." *Evidence to the contrary aside.*

A dark eyebrow shoots up as his gaze settles on my face. I wince and shake my head.

"Sorry, I know you're only trying to help. Being considered helpless is one of my triggers lately. My ex-boyfriend used it as one of the many reasons he broke up with me. Said he didn't want to be stuck taking care of me the rest of his life like my family does."

I press my lips together. Why am I over sharing?

"Your ex sounds like an ass. You're not helpless and families take care of one another. Just because you accept help from time to time does not make you helpless. I don't know where I'd be without my family."

Ron taps me on the tip of my nose with his glove covered finger. "Don't let someone else tell you who you are."

"You're right, of course. Sometimes it's hard to remember." Especially when someone you thought loved you and wanted to spend the rest of his life with you, dumps you and tears a giant hole in your reality.

"I better get back to work. You need to get in your car and warm up." He opens my door for me. The door makes an ominous creak like it's protesting the cold as much as I am.

"Thank you." I slide onto my seat and grip the steering wheel.

"You're welcome and please get your tires changed. I don't want to worry about you driving on these."

"I will. It's on my list." I tap the side of my head.

He shuts my door and lifts his hand in a wave before turning away.

Once I'm no longer in his line of sight, I wobble from side to side yanking on my coat that has somehow managed to wrap around me like a tourniquet. I bang my head on the ceiling and smash my hand against the console when my coat finally slips free.

A knock on my window has me squeezing my eyes closed and praying Ron didn't witness my undignified wrestling match with my coat.

I peek out the window and let out a sigh of relief. Monica's grinning face instead of Ron's fills my vision.

I press the button and lower the window. "Hey."

"Hi. Everything okay in there?"

"I suppose it was too much to hope that you didn't witness that?"

"Afraid so. I wasn't sure if you spotted a spider in your car or if you were rocking out to some music blasting through your headphones. But then I saw you weren't wearing any, and I didn't hear any music so..."

"Just a wrestling match with my coat."

"Been there, done that. Where are you off to today? You're usually one of the last stragglers leaving the building."

"Dentist appointment. Which I better get going to, or I'll be late."

"Okay." Monica taps her hand against my open window. "We'll chat later. We're still on for book club next week, right?"

"Definitely. Oh, I meant to suggest it last month, but it doesn't seem fair for you to always host it at your house. We can rotate each month so it's not always on you. My apartment isn't big, but it can fit the handful of us."

"I don't mind hosting, but I also wouldn't mind taking turns either." She chuckles. "We can see what everyone thinks next week. Did you read Aggie's book selection, yet?"

"Boy did I. I don't think I've ever blushed so hard in my life and that was just while reading a book!"

Monica throws her head back and laughs. "Yeah, it was pretty darn steamy. The discussion should be interesting."

"I'll probably be bright red the entire time. I don't consider myself a prude, but I may need to reassess if that's the sort of book your aunt reads."

"Hey, you can learn a lot from books. I admit that she surprised me with her choice. I'd say it makes me see her and my uncle in a whole new light, but I don't wish to go there...ever."

I laugh and shake my head. "I really need to go, but book club will be fun."

Monica backs away while I close my window, put on my seatbelt, and put the car in drive. I wave as I drive away.

Book club has been more fun than I thought it would be. I agreed to join because I needed to develop a social life, but getting together every month with Monica, Kerry, Aggie, and Sally has been a blast. I read a lot anyway and now I get to hear other perspectives on the books. Someone always points out things that I didn't even notice. Aggie and Sally are both around my grandparents' age, but they don't act like my grandmothers. I think it would be embarrassing discussing the steamy romance books with my grandmothers, but Aggie and Sally are so open and honest it's comfortable. I never would've guessed my former high school English teacher was such a hoot to hang out with. Just goes to show you that you never really know someone until you spend time with them outside of work. It's a shame Sally retired, she was one of the best teachers, but she deserves to rest.

I step on the brake for the stop sign ahead and my tires slip and lose traction. My breath lodges somewhere in my throat as the car slides. It comes to a stop and I huff out the breath I was holding. *Yep, definitely time for new tires.*

I'll make an appointment while I wait at the dentist's office. My chest is tight as I turn onto Main Street. The park on the left is a wide field of white with a few bare trees in the middle and the frozen lake beyond. Fishing huts dot the icy expanse. Freezing my butt off sitting in one of those huts to catch a fish through a hole in the ice is not my idea of a good time, but Dad and Carter go every year.

A shiver dances up my spine and I crank the heat up a notch. My tires slip again as I turn into the parking lot of the dentist. Getting into an accident because of worn tires would give a little too much proof to Jack's criticisms. Helpless, forgetful, spoiled...what else did he accuse me of? Oh yes, he called me a slob.

Jerk! I forget things, like checking the time. Time management is not one of my strengths. But I'm not spoiled or a slob. I'm no neat freak, but it's not like my apartment is unhygienic or anything. And I pay my own way. I have a job. I take care of myself.

Slapping the top of the steering wheel, I grit my back teeth together. Why am I thinking about Jack again? He's in my past and that's where he needs to stay buried.

Preferably six feet under.

I wince and glance upward. *I didn't mean that!* Much.

Ron's right, Jack is an ass. Why didn't I see it before? How could I have wanted to marry him? He always nitpicked me in his passive aggressive way. He would criticize me and then laugh it off like it was a joke. Not funny.

And there I go, thinking about him again. Why did I mention him to Ron? If he did have any romantic interest in me, now he'll probably think I'm still hung up on my ex.

Kind of like I believe he's still in love with his wife?

No, not the same at all. He's a widow. I've never married, and apparently I was in a deluded one-sided relationship with someone who didn't even like me—never mind love me.

Chapter Six

H ope's eyes drift close as I finish reading the sentence. I smile and close the book. She had me read it three times. Apparently, it's her favorite bedtime book. She sighs softly as I tuck the blanket around her. I turn off her bedside lamp and ease out of her room.

Gran fell on ice in her driveway today so Mom asked me to fill in for her and babysit Hope. I hesitated only for a moment. Keeping a professional distance with boundaries is important but living and working in such a small town makes it impossible not to know or even be related to the students at times. Our substitute teachers are often parents of the students and while I haven't had any of my little second cousins in my class, the first-grade team works together often so I have taught them. Besides, I love spending time with Hope. She's such a sweetheart.

I leave her door open a few inches in case she wakes and needs me and tiptoe down the hall and down the few steps to the living room. The contemporary style house Ron and Hope live in is only a few miles down the road from my parents' house and my apartment. In the warmer months, I could walk or even jog the distance easily. That's if I ever start the jogging program I keep promising myself to begin. Timmy and Tommy's mom, Olivia, sent me a link for an app that teaches you how to start running by intermittently walking and jogging in longer increments. She claims jogging is her *me* time, but I can't muster up any enthusiasm for the activity. My *me* time involves curling up with a good book or reclining in the hammock in my parents' backyard. Neither of which burn any calories, however.

There's a photograph of Ron, Hope, and I assume her mother on the mantel. They appear so happy. They're all smiling with their arms around each other. Ruth was beautiful—tall, blonde, obviously athletic by her toned muscles.

Sighing, I wander around the room. There's a few more photographs of Hope and I guess her grandparents. I'd peeked into the open rooms earlier while playing hide and seek with Hope. Either Ron is a bit of a neat freak, or he'd cleaned up ahead of my arrival. There were no piles of laundry, dirty dishes, or random toys cluttering any of the rooms. I made sure Mom cleared the babysitting switch with him ahead of time, so he wasn't surprised having me show up at his door.

He hadn't been the slightest bit awkward having me babysit his daughter while he went out on a date. If that didn't tell me firmly that his innocent flirtations with me meant nothing, I don't know what would.

Is this his first date, or has he been dating the woman for a while? If he was dating her at Christmas and kissed me like he did, then my opinion of him is going to drop. I suppose if they're not exclusive then I can't judge. It could be any one of the half a dozen single moms that swarm around him at school—or even one of the single teachers that are always giggling when he's around. Anyone but Lisette, he must have better taste than that. Sure, she's attractive, but cold and disdainful. At least around me anyway.

Of course it could be a woman he met at work or on a dating app. Jen keeps trying to get me to make a profile and join one. Wouldn't it be ironic if Ron and I got matched up on one? I'm probably not his type. He's pointed out our age difference and judging by the picture of Hope's mom, I'm several inches and attractive points shy of his type.

I pour myself a glass of water in the kitchen and lean against the gray granite countertop. Jen goes on dates from dating apps all the time. But then again, she calls them hook ups, not dates, for a reason. My sister is not looking for a relationship, just a temporary bedmate. I could never do that. I need to know a guy and feel comfortable with him before I would even consider having sex with him. I probably should've waited longer than the year I did with Jack. Like, never. He was my first and only. How am I ever supposed to be that intimate with another guy? I thought I'd marry him. Look how wrong I was.

Headlights shine against the front windows. I glance at the time. It's not even nine o'clock. Did the date not go well?

Oh God, he's not bringing her back here, is he? I lurch away from the counter and then sag back.

It's his house. He's free to do whatever he likes. It's none of my business.

The front door clicks open. I place my glass on the counter and chew on my lip. What should I do? Should I sit at the table?

Too late he's already walking across the living room. I certainly don't want him to see me jumping in a chair or falling to the floor after I trip over my own two feet trying to look nonchalant.

His profile appears in the archway. He's glancing down the hall to the bedrooms. There's no one with him. His head swivels and his gaze lands on me standing in the middle of the kitchen.

"Hey."

"Hope is asleep."

He nods as he walks into the kitchen. "Everything go all right?"

"She was a perfect angel."

Ron stops a foot away from me. "Thanks for filling in for your mom. I hope your grandmother is okay."

"She's fine. Mom called about two hours ago and said she didn't break anything when she fell, just sore and bruised."

"That's good."

"Well, I'll get out of your way." I step to the right and head towards the living room to grab my coat off the back of the couch.

"Hold up."

I glance over my shoulder.

"Let me pay you before you scurry off."

"On the house." I wave him off. It was only three hours and I'm not comfortable taking money from him for watching Hope. I snatch my coat off the couch and stuff my arms inside the sleeves.

"Hey, wait a minute, will you? What's the rush?" He pulls out his wallet.

I jam my hat on my head and pull my gloves out of my other pocket. They fall to the floor and I squat down and swipe one off the floor as Ron picks up the other and hands it to me.

"Thanks."

"I'm glad to see you're wearing gloves this time." He taps me on the end of my nose.

I swipe at his hand and pull away. "I'm not a kid."

"I'm well aware."

I glance up at his face. His gaze travels over my body and back up. Good thing I changed out of the sweatshirt and joggers I was wearing when Mom called. The blue sweater and jeans I picked might not be overtly sexy, but they're form fitting enough to show I have some curves.

"Then why do you treat me like one?"

He puts his hands in his pockets. "In what way do I treat you like a kid?"

"The taps on the nose. The reminders about gloves." I wave the glove in the air. "The references to our age difference."

The corner of his lips quirk up. "The age references are a reminder to myself. The others are a poor attempt at flirting. I guess I'm rustier than I thought."

"Oh." He was flirting with me? "A reminder for what?"

"That you're too young for me."

"So you *do* see me as a kid."

"No, I just feel old compared to you. You have your whole life ahead of you."

"So do you."

He rubs the back of his neck. "Doesn't feel like it."

"Ten years isn't much."

He smiles. "Depends how you look at it."

"I suppose your date is the same age as you?"

"What date?" His frown clears into a smile. "You thought I was on a date?"

"Weren't you? I mean it's none of my business if you were." Great, now he knows I've been wondering.

"It was a work event, not a date."

"Oh." Why does it suddenly feel like fireworks are bursting inside me in a kaleidoscope of colors and sound?

"Is that why you've been so snippy tonight?"

"Snippy? I'm not snippy." Reserved and professional is not snippy.

"You haven't been your cheerful and charming self."

He thinks I'm cheerful and charming?

He grins. "There's the smile I was missing."

I touch my cheek. He's right, I'm smiling. My cheeks warm beneath my fingers.

"You're like a happy sprite, always smiling and making those around you happy."

I narrow my eyes. "Is that a dig on my height?"

"No, I think you're the perfect size." He raises his hand and tucks my hair behind my ear. His fingers trace the outer shell of my ear and down to my jaw.

All thoughts fly out of my head as my gaze drops to his lips. His head lowers slowly like he's giving me every chance to move away.

I go up on tiptoe and meet him halfway. Our lips touch and my body sighs. Yes, this is what I wanted.

I grasp the lapels of his coat and tug him closer.

One hand cradles my jaw while the other clasps my waist. His fingers span half my lower back while his thumb strokes my side.

His tongue seeks mine as our kiss deepens. Butterflies take flight inside me. I loop my hands behind his neck. His soft hair brushes over my fingers.

Both his hands grip my sides and put a distance between us. My mouth trails after his, but he lifts his head.

"We need to slow down."

Do we?

He licks his lips. The light reflects in his glasses. He squeezes my waist and drops his hands.

I snatch my hands off him to my chest and stare at the floor. Did I entirely misread the situation?

He kissed me. I might have leaned toward him inviting his kiss, but he definitely kissed me. It's not like I jumped him or anything.

"You're Hope's teacher and her babysitter's daughter. I won't complicate either of those situations."

"Okay." I understand—sort of. "What do you want to do?"

Ron rubs both hands over his face. "What I want isn't an option here. I have to put Hope first. You understand that, right?"

"Of course."

He nods. "I'll walk you out."

So, slow down actually means stop.

"That's not necessary." I toss an absent smile in his direction and grab the door handle.

"Wait."

Ron bends over and picks up my gloves off the floor. I must have dropped them during the kiss.

"Thanks."

"Tina..."

I glance back, but he simply stares. I give him a tight smile and walk out the door.

The cold air hits me like a slap as I hurry to my car with my coat flapping in the wind. I scowl down at the fashionable ankle boots I wore instead of warm, sensible, ones. My humiliation will be complete if I slip and fall on my ass.

When am I going to learn? I should've kept my mouth closed. How am I ever going to face him again?

Chapter Seven

"You have an incoming call."

I press the phone button on my steering wheel. It's probably Monica wondering where I am. I was supposed to be at Aggie's house for book club fifteen minutes ago.

"Tina?"

Jack?!

My gaze drops to the display. Why the heck didn't I check before I answered?

A horn blares and I jerk my gaze back up to the road. Headlights from an oncoming car zoom towards me.

I've drifted over the line!

I yank the steering wheel to the right. A deer crossing sign looms in front of me and my headlights shine on the foot of snow still lining the road. I turn back to the left a little less aggressively and straighten my car in my own lane.

"Tina? Are you there? What's going on? Are you driving?"

I glance down at the button. I could just disconnect the call without saying a word. He might think the call dropped out.

Then he could leave a voicemail and I could prepare myself for talking to him and know what I'm going to say.

"You didn't cause an accident, did you?"

No, no thanks to you!

"Tina? Stop ignoring me. It's childish."

Well, shit!

If I hang up now, he'll think I proved him right. I pull into the closest driveway and put my car in park. No way do I trust myself driving while dealing with him.

"Why are you calling me, Jack?"

"I wanted to talk to you. I miss you. Did you pull over? You know how distracted you get."

I should've hung up as soon as I heard his voice. I don't always get distracted—just when my ex calls unexpectedly and I haven't talked to him since he moved away and dumped me over the phone.

"It's been seven months, Jack. Why are you calling me now?" Not that I'm counting or anything, but it's kind of hard not to when he did it right before school started.

"I told you. I miss you. What's new? How's work? Your family?"

"It's March. I'm already preparing my students for next year in second grade. Mom and Dad are good. Mom was bored in retirement so she babysits part-time. Dad is still mumbling about the possibility of retirement but we doubt he ever will. Carter just got a promotion at work for something to do with a new software program, but I don't understand anything when he starts talking in computer language. Jen is the same. She still hates you."

"Do you?"

Tears fill my eyes as I peer at the house perched at the end of the random driveway I'm parked in. I hope the owners don't call the cops and report me as a trespasser.

"You hurt me, Jack. But I don't hate you."

Intense disliking faded to a disenchanted melancholy a few months back. There was a time when I desperately craved him to call me and tell me he missed me.

"I couldn't pass up the opportunity here in California. You must see that."

"How can I see anything when you never told me you were even thinking about moving let alone applying for a job across the country? I didn't know about it until after you'd already accepted the position and moved out of your apartment."

And you never asked me to go with you—not once.

"This is why, right here. You're getting all worked up and only seeing your side of it. You had our entire future planned out in Granite Cove. That's not what I wanted."

"Clearly! It would have been nice if you mentioned it to me instead of letting me blissfully go along thinking everything was great."

"You never asked if it was what I wanted. It all revolved around you and what you wanted."

My mouth opens and closes and I shake my head. Am I really so selfish and self-centered?

I dash the tears off my cheeks with the palms of my hands.

We had several conversations about our future together over the course of our relationship. He even made a joke once about our kids going to school where their mother taught and how there would be positives and negatives on both sides. Not once did he say he wanted something different.

"Why don't you come out to California for a visit? You have spring break coming up."

I gawk at his phone number on the display as if it's his face in front of me. *Is he serious?* He just blamed me for the end of our relationship and basically said I'm an awful, selfish human being. And now he's asking me to visit him in California?

Typical, really. He accepts no responsibility for his actions or his part.

"The weather is perfect. I bet you still have snow on the ground there. We could go to the beach here."

He wants me back and I feel...nothing. Not even vindication. Just hollow. He truly means nothing to me. Jack is part of my past.

"No thanks."

"No to the beach. No to spring break? Or no to California and me all together?"

"I sincerely wish you all the best, Jack, but we're over and have been for some time. If you loved me like you claimed, you never would've treated me the way you did. And you certainly wouldn't have tried blaming me for it all. Goodbye."

Not caring to hear his response, I hit the disconnect button just as the outside lights on the house turn on.

I back out of their driveway with a wince and a sorry wave—not that they can see or interpret my intentions.

A smile twitches my lips as I drive away. The weight of Jack has been figuratively lifted from my shoulders. I have closure.

Yeah, it was a nice little ego boost to have him call missing me. I'm glad I picked up after all. It wasn't so nice hearing him trying to shift the blame all on me, but what a moment of clarity. That's exactly what he does. He'd have me doubting myself and feeling awful and I would end up apologizing to him and trying to make amends. Nope, not going to happen. His tricks don't work with me anymore.

I peer at the clock and wince. I'm really late now. Is a half hour too late to still show up?

Aggie's house should be here somewhere. She said it was a white raised ranch, and I'd have no trouble finding it because her husband had spotlights on every corner of the house and his garage in back.

Ah, there it is. That must be it. It is indeed lit up. I don't think the house can be seen from space like Aggie joked, but it does make it easier to locate. I inch along the driveway and park behind Monica's car. I'm sure they won't mind I'm so late. Book club is casual and none of the women here are the type to make a big deal out of my tardiness.

The brick pathway to the door is free from any snow or ice. I breathe a quick sigh of relief. I'm still wearing the flats I wore at school today. At least I remembered to wear boots to school and change into my flats when I got to my classroom. The problem is I forgot to change back into my boots before I left and the slush in the school parking lot oozed over the tops of my shoes. My feet are doing a great impression of blocks of ice despite the heat I blasted on them on the way over here.

Aggie's familiar cackle drifts out the door as I raise my hand and knock. The door swings open, revealing an older man with a round, red, face and puffs of white hair sticking up around his head.

"You here for the club thingy?"

"Um, book club, yes. I'm Tina Cooper."

"Come in. Come in. Don't let all the heat out. I'm Dennis, Aggie's husband. They're all up there in the living room." He points up as I step inside. There are a few stairs and a railing separating us.

Kerry peaks over the back of a chair against the railing. "Hi, Tina."

I smile and wave. Aggie stands and peers down. "Get on up here girl. Dennis get her some wine."

He nods next to me after he shuts the door. I open my mouth to decline, but then close it. Why not? I could use some tonight.

"You can hang your coat up there. I'll bring you the wine." He shuffles up the stairs after pointing to the coat tree.

After hanging up my coat, I join the ladies upstairs. "I'm sorry I'm late. What did I miss?"

Monica pats the couch next to her. "Not too much. Aggie thinks the heroine is an idiot and her and Sally have been arguing about it."

"We're not arguing, we're discussing." Aggie winks and Sally rolls her eyes.

"I'm simply saying we have a different perspective and even though we can see how bad he is for her, Katarina can't. She's in love and trying to make it work." Sally folds her arms over her chest and raises her chin.

I murmur, "thank you," when Dennis hands me a glass of wine.

"What do you think, Uncle Dennis?"

His widened eyes stare at Monica for a moment before he glances at his wife. "I think the T.V. is calling my name." He shuffles out of sight remarkably fast.

Monica chuckles and leans over to me. "He hung around for the first ten minutes or so until Aunt Aggie brought up one of the sex scenes. His face got redder and redder until he simply disappeared without a word."

"Wait, did I read the wrong book? There were no sex scenes in it." Sally chose a historical book this month. At least, I thought she did. We were supposed to meet at her house, but she was having her floors refinished so Aggie volunteered. Or did I get that all mixed up?

"No, there weren't. She described one from the January pick."

"Oh, well that explains it. I turned red just reading them."

"She knew he wouldn't stick around."

"Poor guy—run out of his own living room."

"Don't feel too bad for him. When he's not in his garage, his happiest place is in front of the T.V. in the den."

"Ain't that the truth." Aggie leans over and pats the arm of Sally's chair. "Don't get your feathers ruffled. I just can't understand how she believed anything coming out of that man's mouth or why she went back to him time and again."

"It was a different time period and culture." Kerry taps her finger against her glass. "I think we need to keep that in mind."

Monica turns her head and looks at me. "What did you think of the book, Tina?"

I finish my sip of red wine and cross my legs. "I agree with all of you. Kerry is right about it being a different time and culture, but so is Sally. It is hard to have a clear perspective when it's happening to you. But Aggie's right too. Katarina was a bit of an idiot for going back to him." I shake my head and stare into my glass. "Speaking from personal experience, I wonder how I couldn't see the red flags in my relationship. I feel stupid for only realizing it now and not back then. I believed what he told me and never questioned what he didn't."

Every eye is on me full of sympathy and confusion. "My ex called me on my way here and said he missed me in one breath and placed the blame for our breakup on me in the next. It blindsided me when he dumped me. I thought he was going to propose. Instead, he moved without telling me and broke up with me over the phone."

Aggie and Sally both gasp. Kerry frowns and shakes her head. Monica is silent next to me, but I know she's already heard the story around school. We've never discussed it, but at the beginning of the school year she told me she was there for me if I wanted to talk or even go to an axe throwing class and release some aggression.

"My point is, even after he dumped me that way, I probably would've taken him back a few months ago. I wanted him to call me and tell me he couldn't live without me. Blah blah blah. It's ridiculous, I know."

Monica squeezes my hand. "It's not ridiculous at all. You were hurt and in love with a guy. It doesn't end in an instant. Feelings linger and it takes time to get perspective."

"Lies of omission are still lies. It sounds like your man was a cowardly liar. Don't let him bully you. You deserve better."

I smile at Sally before taking a sip of wine.

Kerry raises her glass. "I second that. Men really are from a different planet. I don't understand them at all."

"Have to agree on that one too. Men say women are hard to understand, but they're the ones that make little sense." I shake my head. "I swear guys send mixed signals all the time. How are we supposed to know where we stand?"

Ron runs hot one minute and cold the next. I haven't seen or heard from him since our kiss in January. He didn't even make the teacher parent conferences last month. I know the world doesn't revolve around me, but it's hard not to feel like he's purposely avoiding me.

"I went on this date with a guy I met on a dating app. It was not going well in my mind. The guy barely said two words to me. I was grasping for things to say. Yet, the check arrives, and he wants to know if we're going to my place or his. He thought we were going to have sex." Monica holds both hands up. "I said neither and left. He was just there for a hook up, but he gave no indication prior. There are specific apps if that's what he's looking for. I avoid those because of it."

"My sister, Jen, could give you a full list. She's been trying to get me to sign up for one, but it's just not my style."

Kerry pinches the bridge of her nose and drops her head. "Okay, full confession...I filled out a profile a few days ago and I have my first date this weekend. Now I'm wondering if I should cancel and avoid potential disaster."

"Nonsense. You're young. I say live a little. If you never take any chances, then you'll be stuck in place. If I was single, I'd be on every single app or doodad I could find." Aggie jerks her thumb in Sally's direction. "I've been trying to get her to try one for ages, but she'll have none of it."

Sally shakes her head. "I'm done with men. I'm not interested. I had my Herbert, and that was enough for me."

Sally retired from teaching right before her husband got sick. I remember Mom mentioning they were doing a fundraiser at school while I was in college. Is that how Ron feels too as a widower? He had one love, and that was sufficient?

Hope is as sweet as ever. She brought up our pizza challenge last week, and I had no idea what to say to her. When Ron said he wanted to slow down and not complicate the teacher daughter situation, what he really must have meant was he wanted no contact whatsoever. Why couldn't he have just said he wasn't interested? And why did he kiss me?

Oh Lord! Was the kiss so bad he changed his mind? Am I bad kisser?

"What's that look for?"

I glance at Monica and then around the room. Sally and Aggie are murmuring to each other and Kerry just walked into the bathroom. I lean over to Monica and whisper, "this guy kissed me and he's ghosted me ever since. It just occurred to me that I might be a terrible kisser."

"I feel fairly confident in saying I doubt that is it. I've never kissed you, obviously. But you've been in relationships and kissed other guys. None of them have ever complained, have they?"

"No, but it hasn't been all that many. I'm only twenty-five. What if they were all too nice to say?"

"How long were you with your ex?"

"Almost three years."

"Is he the type of guy who would have kept that to himself?"

Would he have? He apparently kept plenty of secrets from me. He never complained about my kissing technique. Is that something he would've ignored?

"No, he would've made a joke about it. Joking was his passive aggressive way of criticizing me."

"What a jerk. You're well rid of him and you have your answer. You're not a bad kisser." She leans her head closer. "Does this have anything to do with a certain single dad that has all the single women at school in a tizzy this year?"

I suck in a sharp breath.

"I'll take that as a yes."

How did she know? Did I give myself away somehow? Do I stare after him like a puppy or something?

Oh crap! Has he been kissing a lot of women? Am I that clueless?

He said he wasn't on a date that night I babysat, but he didn't say he wasn't dating at all.

"Breathe Tina, your secret is safe with me."

"How did you know?"

"I've seen you two looking at each other. He's tolerant of the women flirting with him, but he doesn't encourage them. He seeks you out like the women seeking him out."

I let out a sigh and open and close the clasp on my watch. That's good to know, but is it true?

"I'm his daughter's teacher."

"Are you saying that because you think it's taboo dating him or as a reason he seeks you out?"

"Both, I guess."

"There's no rule against dating a parent and he doesn't look at you like you're his daughter's teacher. At least, I've never had a parent look at me that way."

"But he's been avoiding me. He didn't even schedule a conference."

"Have you asked him? So many misunderstandings can be resolved with an honest conversation."

Ugh. "You're right. I know you're right, but I don't think I'm ready to open myself up to more heartbreak right now."

"But you'll never know if it's heartbreak if you don't ask."

Chapter Eight

A dozen cupcakes with kitten faces sit in a container on the counter. Little black whiskers, tiny pink triangles for noses, and slanted yellow eyes decorate each one.

"Mom, who are these kitten cupcakes for?"

"Oh good, you can tell what they are. I was worried people would think they were rabbits or not be able to tell they're animals at all. Art has never been one of my talents." She peeks over my shoulder. "They're for Hope. She's been trying to convince Ron to get her a kitten."

I whirl around and lean back against the counter. "I thought you said they weren't coming?"

"Who?" Mom opens a drawer and pulls out a handful of serving spoons.

"Ron and Hope,"

"Oh, they weren't, but Ron told me yesterday they could make it after all. Would you make sure your father filled the coolers with ice?"

I glance out the kitchen window to the deck. "Sure."

Ron and Hope are coming? I shove open the slider. A line of coolers sit on the far side of the deck. Hope didn't say anything to me in class, but I suppose she wouldn't have known if Ron just decided yesterday. I guess he's done avoiding me.

Now I wish I'd taken Monica's advice and talked to him. At least to clear the air. I don't know how I feel about Ron. Yes, I'm attracted—all right very attracted. But is it any more than that? I didn't want to risk humiliation or heartbreak if it's not. Besides, there's Hope to consider too. I would never do anything to hurt Hope.

Will he act like nothing ever happened, or ignore me? No, I can't imagine he'd ignore me at my parents' party.

Dad steps out of the garage carrying a bag of ice in each arm. "She sent you out here to check up on me, didn't she?"

"She sure did."

"Whatever possessed your mother to throw a Memorial Day party?"

"She said it's been too long since the whole family got together."

Dad grumbles something under his breath as he empties the ice into the coolers.

"I'll let her know the ice is taken care of and see if she needs help with anything else." He nods.

Jen is in the kitchen with Mom when I step inside. "Hey Sis."

"Hey." She walks over and gives me a one arm hug while munching on a carrot.

"Dad put the ice in the coolers."

Mom glances up from the vegetable platter she's assembling. "I saw." She lifts her head to the window over the sink which looks out over the deck.

"What can I help you with?"

"As I told your sister, everything is done until the guests arrive. When they do, you can help carry food out."

"Looks like Carter brought his own entourage." Jen moseys over to the slider. "And one of them is a girl."

Mom and I turn and look out the window. Carter, two guys, and a woman stand on the deck chatting with Dad.

Mom sucks in a breath. "Do you think she's his girlfriend?"

"Not a chance." Jen walks over to us and leans against the counter with her back to the window. "Even if you ignore the fact that he's never gotten serious enough about a girl to bring her home, check out their body language. They're not touching at all. They're not even leaning towards one another or sneaking glances at each other. If they're having sex—with each other—I'll go skinny dipping in the pond."

I study Carter and the woman. Jen is right they aren't acting like a couple, but they could be doing it on purpose. Maybe they aren't ready for everyone to know. Or this could be some sort of test run of how she is with his family. I could imagine Carter doing something like that. Of course, I could also see him just being friends with her. Actually, that's the more likely scenario.

I glance over at Jen chomping on chips. "You'd go skinny dipping in the pond normally so that's not exactly saying much." The pond out back isn't that large or deep, but it's big enough to cool us off in the summer. I've never had the courage to go skinny dipping, however.

"True." She shrugs. "I have on more than one occasion."

"Yes, but let's not remind your father of the time he caught you and your friends, Tammy and Joe. He wanted to murder Joe and ship you off to a convent." Mom wanders away from the window and over to the fridge.

Jen frowns and stares at the chip in her hand. "Do they even have convents anymore?"

"Of course they do. Where do you think nuns get their training?" Mom places a bowl of salsa on the counter.

Jen points her chip at Mom. "We're not Catholic."

"I believe your father would've converted." Mom sighs and plants her hands on her hips. "Please carry out the appetizers. And be polite. No talk of skinny dipping either."

"You know Joe is gay, right? He couldn't care less about seeing my naked body." Jen pops the chip in her mouth and grabs the salsa and dip while I pour the bags of chips into the empty bowls.

"You do realize that's not the point, right?" Mom shoos us out the door.

Jen mutters, "I bet they wouldn't care if Carter went skinny dipping," as we walk out on the deck.

I frown. Would they? My parents aren't chauvinists. I've never felt like they treated me differently than Carter because of my gender.

"Do you really believe that?"

She gives me a sideways glare as we place the appetizers on the table. Her expression clears as she glances over to Dad.

"No, I'm being defensive."

"Why? It was years ago."

She waves her hand. "It's not that. A client at work made a comment that he wanted a man's perspective on the project I'm working on and it's really got my back up."

"Wow, I'm surprised you restrained yourself."

"Who says I did?"

I bite my lip. Jen has never been one to keep her opinions to herself. I've often wished I had her candor, but I care too much what everyone else thinks. "Jen, what did you do?"

She shrugs. "I only reminded him what century we were living in."

"How did that go over?"

Jen rolls her eyes. "He became even more pompous and my boss fawned all over him until he was appeased."

"You didn't get in trouble with your boss?"

"Please. He knows I'm the best he's got."

I wish I had an ounce or two of her confidence too.

Carter puts an arm around each of our shoulders. "Hey, you two, come meet my friends."

After we meet his friends and carry out the rest of the appetizers, more guests arrive and Mom and Dad mingle. I keep an eye out for Ron and Hope while I do my best to pay attention to the conversations aimed at me.

Will he ignore me? Will he act like nothing has ever happened between us? Will he apologize for avoiding me?

What if he brings a date?

It's not out of the realm of possibility. He could be dating. Would he bring her here to my parents' home where he knows I'm bound to be? That would certainly send a clear message now, wouldn't it?

"Am I really that boring?"

I blink up at Carter's friend. What was his name?

"Of course not! I'm sorry. I guess I'm a little distracted. What were you saying?" And could you work in your name somehow too?

He chuckles. "I was asking if you enjoyed sailing."

"Oh, I don't know. I've never been. You sail?"

"Yes, I grew up sailing. I could take you out next weekend."

Is he asking me out on a date? It certainly sounds like it. "Um..."

"Hey Kev, want a beer?" Carter holds a bottle out.

Kevin, that's his name. He works with my brother. I stare at his blond head as he takes the bottle from Carter with a smile. He's handsome and seems nice enough. What would be the harm in going out with him?

"Would you like a beer?" Kevin tilts the bottle in his hand.

"No thanks, I'm good."

"Tina doesn't like beer."

"Can I get you something else?"

Carter frowns at Kevin.

I shake my head and smile as Carter narrows his eyes at his friend. Oh boy, here we go. Big brother mode is about to kick in. Usually it's Jen he warns his friends to stay away from. I don't think he's ever had to with me. His friends were always older and saw me as the kid sister, but Kevin is a recent addition and didn't know me when I chased after my big brother with pigtails in my hair.

"Miss Cooper!"

Hope runs across the deck and throws her arms around my waist. I hug her back and grin. "Hi Hope, I heard you might come today." My gaze drifts up and I spot Ron. He's chatting with my father over by the grill. His back is to me, but I recognize that shade of hair brushing the collar of the green shirt and the way he stands with his hip cocked to the side.

He turns his head as my mother joins them. I get a hitch in my chest at his profile.

"We brought potato salad."

I turn my attention back to Hope. "I'll be sure to try some. I bet it's yummy."

"Hey munchkin, I happen to be a potato salad expert." Carter tugs on her braid.

She giggles and slips her hand into mine.

"Come on, Kev, there are some relatives you haven't met." Carter latches onto his arm.

Kevin looks at me, down at Hope, and then back at me. "We'll talk more later, right?"

I laugh and nod as Carter drags him away. If he manages to work his way back to me and asks me out, should I say yes? Maybe that's just what I need to stop fixating on Ron.

"Hi."

His voice sends a pool of warmth bubbling inside me. I swallow hard and turn my head to meet his gaze.

Ron hands Hope a juice box and me a ginger ale. He remembered what I drink.

"Hope, I saw Moose looking a little lonely by the stairs over there. Why don't you go say hello?"

"Okay!" Hope runs across the deck and plops down next to Moose on the ground. The Saint Bernard promptly rolls over on his side and presents her with his belly to rub. The constant drool drives my mother crazy, but my father loves that dog like it's one of his children.

"How are you?"

I take a sip of my soda. "Good, you?" Small talk. We're having small talk. I thought he was trying to give us some privacy when he suggested Hope visit the dog, but maybe he truly thought Moose looked lonely.

"What are you doing on June 17th?"

"Um...what? The last day of school?" Does he want to know if I have a party planned for the class? Typically, the last day is a fun day.

"Are you busy that night?"

That night? "I don't think so."

He leans toward me slightly. "Great, it's a date then."

A date? He's asking me out on a date? I stare up at him silently. No mention of the months of silence? He just assumes I'll say yes?

"You'll no longer be my daughter's teacher and I for one would very much like to see where this relationship could go. Do you feel the same?"

My entire body clenches as I stare into his eyes. *Yes! One hundred percent yes!*

I can't say that. It would be too telling. Too forward.

I nod slowly not trusting myself to speak.

A grin spreads over his face. His gaze roams my face for a moment before he clicks his glass against mine. "Until then. I'll be counting the days." He walks away. I whirl around and stare out at the yard so no one will see the euphoria drenching my entire being.

$$Chapter\ Nine$$

What if the date is a total flop? What if we have nothing to talk about? What if he finds me completely uninteresting after waiting so long for our first date? Variations of the same themes have been running through my mind more and more as the date got closer. Now that it's here, I feel like I'm going to vomit.

I twirl the large, gold, hoop, earring around and around the clasp as I stare at the entrance to the parking lot. I told Ron it would be more convenient if I met him at the restaurant rather than have him pick me up at my apartment, but I doubt if I fooled him. Living over my parents' garage has disadvantages. One of them being that the chances of them not noticing Ron picking me up for a date are slim to none. If they knew, there would be questions, comments, and advice.

Ron and I need a chance to figure out if this is going anywhere before we have to deal with anyone else knowing and weighing in.

A car pulls in, but it's not his. For once in my life, I'm early. Who knew excessive nerves could prompt me to be on time? I tug the hemline of my green dress closer to my knees but with every movement it inches back up. What possessed me to purchase something so daring? I've never worn such a short, form fitting, dress before.

Of course I know what possessed me, I wanted to be sexy. Instead, I feel exposed and ridiculous.

I'll have to remember to keep my knees glued together or risk exposing a heck of a lot more. I glance down at my newfound abundance of cleavage thanks to the new pushup bra I bought with the dress. I better not bend over too far either.

Why am I pretending to be someone I'm not? I'll probably break something or at the very least fall and make a fool of myself trying to walk on these stilts instead of shoes I splurged on. I practiced walking in the three-inch heels in my apartment all week, but I still have to stare at my feet or I end up twisting my ankle and falling over. Instead of a sexy, hip swaying strut, all I can do is inch along like I'm trying to traverse a balance beam.

The poor guy will probably run in the other direction when he sees me.

No, Ron is too kind to do that. He'll be courteous and polite.

My gaze darts to the clock on my dashboard. There isn't enough time to go home and change. I look in the rearview mirror. Didn't I toss a cardigan in the backseat last week? It was an unseasonably muggy day, so I took off my sweater on the way home from school. I don't remember taking it out of the car and it was an ivory color so I might be able to pull it off with the green dress.

I stretch my arm back and shove a tote and paper bag out of the way, but there's nothing resembling the cardigan. Twisting in my seat, and perching on my knees, I hang over the console between the two front seats. I snag a piece of material jammed under my seat.

It's a yellow T-shirt with Granite Cove Elementary blazoned across the front, not an ivory cardigan. I don't think I'm willing to risk such a fashion faux pau. I stretch farther wedging my hips firmly between the seats and shove books and papers out of the way. Maybe the sweater slipped underneath somehow. Although, I can't remember the last time I cleaned my car out and if I tossed the sweater here last week, then it should be closer to the top of this mess.

Someone knocks on my driver side window.

I smack my head on the roof and twist towards the sound.

Oh, please, please, don't let it be Ron witnessing my graceless search! My butt is in the air and God only knows what I'm exposing in this position.

I surge backwards only for my shoulders to hit the seats and stop me short. *Good Lord, please don't let me be stuck here!*

Ron's face appears in the back window next to me. I close my eyes and push off the back seat. After several twists and shoves, I land back in the front seat still on my knees. My face is on fire and the flames of mortification are spreading down my neck and chest. How can I extricate myself from this with my dignity intact?

He opens the door and peeks in. "Hi there. Everything okay?" He's grinning.

I suppose it's better than him laughing out right or making a snarky comment like Jack would have done.

"I was...um...looking for a sweater."

He glances towards the back of my car. "Want me to look?"

"No!" Have him see what a slob I can be? No, thank you. "I mean, I must have been mistaken in thinking it was back there."

I shift forward and freeze. How am I supposed to untangle myself from the car without falling flat on my face, exposing myself, or looking like a graceless buffoon?

Let's be honest, the ship has definitely sailed on the last one.

Sighing, I grab hold of the steering wheel with one hand and the back of the seat with my other and lift myself enough to pry one foot and then the other from underneath me. A heel gets lodged between the seat and console.

Laughter bubbles up my throat and spills out. It's either that or cry. I'm now stuck with one foot on the floor and one twisted beneath me while I hold myself up. If my dress climbs any higher on my thighs, Ron will see the beige shapewear smoothing my hips and stomach. Not the greatest first date impression.

An arm reaches past me and dislodges my shoe. Ron's smiling face is inches from my own.

"There we go." He holds out a hand for me to take as he eases out of the car.

I plop my butt down on the seat and swing both legs out before taking his hand. "Thank you."

I teeter in front of him. His warm hand engulfs mine. I slap my other hand against my car before I fall back inside.

Ron steps closer, slips his arm around my waist, and steadies me. "Okay?"

I close my eyes and sigh heavily. "Not really, I have no idea how people manage walking in these things. Or wear this stupid dress." Now that I'm steady, I use my free hand and yank it down from where it has risen to the tops of my thighs. I shake my head. "I'm sorry."

This date is already an epic disaster and we haven't even made it inside the restaurant.

"Why are you apologizing? You look gorgeous and I'm flattered if you wore this for me, but I'd much rather you be comfortable. I don't want you to be miserable, Tina."

He looks over at the restaurant behind him and back to me. "How about we save this place for another date and tonight we pick up some takeout from Billings Creamery? You can take off those torture devices disguised as shoes and I've got a hoodie in my car you can wear if you want. We could have a picnic in my car in front of the lake. Would that make you more comfortable?"

That sounds like heaven! "You wouldn't mind?"

"Are you kidding? Having a gorgeous woman all to myself with no interruptions, fried food, and a view of the lake? It sounds like a perfect date to me."

Ron bends down and clasps my ankle. "Lift."

As I do, he slips off my shoe and does the same to my other foot and tosses the shoes into my car.

"You need anything from in there?"

"Um, my keys and purse." I turn to grab them.

"I got it." Ron leans past me and takes the keys from the ignition and grabs my purse from the passenger seat. "This all?"

I nod as he hands them to me. He hits the button and locks the doors.

How am I going to walk across the parking lot without slicing open my feet on broken glass or something? I slip my keys into my purse and look for his car. As long as I watch where I'm going, I'll be fine. I used to run around barefoot all the time as a kid and it's certainly better than breaking my ankle trying to walk in high heels.

Ron shuts my door and scoops me up in his arms.

I let out a yelp and grab his shoulders. "What are you doing?" The strap of my purse pulls against my wrist like it's telling me to get my feet back on solid ground.

He shifts me higher against his chest and I curl my arms around his neck and hang on for dear life. No one has carried me since I was a kid. Not unless you count Carter throwing me in the pond a few years ago.

"I'd rather not spoil our date with a trip to the hospital because you need stitches or a tetanus shot from whatever is lurking in this parking lot. Besides, it gives me the perfect excuse to hold you in my arms." He winks at me as he strides across to his car in the next row.

My knight in shining armor. Maybe this date is off to the perfect start after all.

Chapter Ten

"I come bearing gifts." Ron sets down a large cardboard box before he sits on the ground next to Hope and me. "There's a bunch of scrap pieces from the deck I had built last summer." He takes out a few varying lengths of composite decking. "I've even got some spindles from the old deck. I'm not sure what you can do with these." He stares at the three-foot-long piece in his hands with a frown.

"Where's your imagination?" I snag the piece out of his hand. "It's a perfect wall for our fairy village, of course."

Hope sucks in a breath and looks at the box. "Do you have more, Daddy? The wall needs to go all around to keep the fairies safe."

Ron hands over a few more pieces of varying lengths. "You make an excellent security chief, or should I say knight?"

Hope giggles. "Miss Cooper said I can be an arky...arkyteck." She scrunches her nose and looks at me. "Is that right?"

"Architect."

Ron chuckles. "That too."

I smile and help her place the wall around the fairy village while Ron takes out more of the deck pieces. Should I tell her it's okay to call me Tina, or would that be awkward? I'm no longer her teacher and I'm dating her father. I'm not sure Ron has told her that, though. It might confuse her. Besides, she'll still see me in the halls at school next year and it would be strange if she called me Tina instead of Miss Cooper there. He's her father so I'll follow his lead.

This is only our first date with Hope present. We've gone out at least once a week since school let out last month, but it's always been just the two of us. It's an odd situation. I'm sure it's normal for him to want to keep some distance between a woman he's newly dating and his daughter. But as her former teacher, obviously I already know Hope. There's also the fact that my mother babysits her during the days and I often see her there. So I wondered when he would include Hope on one of our dates. Now that he has, I can't help being a little nervous. Hope and my dynamic has changed. Yet has it if he hasn't told her anything? She hasn't treated me any different.

When I arrived today, she asked me to watch her swing on the playscape so we went outside and then she spotted a patch of purple flowers under these two trees. I said it looked like a fairy ring and somehow, we ended up making a village for the fairies.

"Okay, master builder, what do you think of this for a fairy house?" Ron has used the deck pieces to form a lopsided building.

Hope stares at the house with her lips pursed. "How will they get in, Daddy? There's no door or windows."

"Hmm, didn't think of that." He removes a front piece and they all collapse. "Guess that won't work."

I grab a few pieces of similar sizes and make a three-sided house with a roof. "There, they can get in and out." I make another one, but triangle shaped.

Hope claps her hands and places some small sticks and rocks in front of the house, forming a pathway.

Ron rests his arm on his bent knee. "Clearly, I am useless here. How about I go into town and grab a pizza for our dinner while you two finish the village?"

He meets my gaze and raises an eyebrow.

Is he asking my opinion on the pizza or if it's okay with me to watch Hope?

She gives him a quick hug. "Okay, Daddy. Bye, love you."

He laughs and hugs her back. "Love you, sweetheart."

Hope crawls over to the box and digs through the contents.

Ron leans towards me. "This okay with you?"

"Of course. Hope and I have the Swanson fairy village under control."

He stands and dusts off his hands. "I'll be back soon."

He doesn't kiss me goodbye.

Of course he wouldn't in front of Hope. I watch him until he disappears into the back of the house. Ron hasn't pressured me at all to have sex. He always ends any embrace we have before it goes too far. Is he being cautious and respectful, or is he not ready or interested in going to the next level?

What if he's waiting for some sort of signal from me? I don't have a clue what that signal could be short of jumping him the next time he kisses me. But what if he's not waiting for me? How mortifying would it be if he tells me no?

Jack is the only man I've ever had sex with and he always had suggestions to improve our encounters so that sometimes it felt like a teaching lesson rather than a passionate expression of our love. What if I suck at sex?

Then again, Ron started dating his wife while they were still in high school. Was she his first and only? It's possible. And if she was, maybe he's nervous too.

Hope puts her hand on my knee. "Do you not want to build fairy houses anymore?"

"I'm sorry honey, my mind was wandering. How about if we build a town hall for the fairies to gather in right in the center of the village?"

"Okay!" She jumps up and grabs pieces from the box.

We use the deck pieces and rocks to make a somewhat circular building in the middle and decorate it with moss, twigs, and leaves.

I snap a few pictures of the village and Hope. "The fairies won't be able to resist this village."

She scoots over and rests her head against my arm as I show her the pictures. "They need a playground!"

"Ooh, that's a clever idea. We'll need some more sticks."

"I'll get them." She jumps up and gathers sticks from under the trees.

A man and a woman stroll around the corner of the house. I stand and dust off the back of my shorts. They're an older couple. The man is bald with a white mustache and the woman has blonde, shoulder length, hair. They look vaguely familiar, but I can't place them. Have I seen them around town?

"Hope!" The woman smiles and waves.

Hope whirls around and a wide grin stretches across her face before she breaks into a run. "Nana! Pop!"

They're Hope's grandparents. Of course, there are pictures of them in the house. But which ones? Ron's parents, or his wife's?

I finger the small diamond stud in my ear that my parents gave me when I graduated from college with my master's degree. I'm not sure which is more terrifying, meeting the parents of the guy I'm dating for the first time, or the parents of his deceased wife.

The woman and man both engulf Hope in hugs and smiles and listen as she chatters away at them. The man keeps glancing at my approach. The woman has yet to look in my direction. How slowly can I walk over there? Ron hasn't been gone long enough to get to town, pick up pizzas, and drive back. How am I supposed to introduce myself to them? Has he mentioned me?

Is that why they're here? He certainly didn't mention they were coming. Are they surprising him because he mentioned he was dating someone?

"Hello." Nana casts a small smile in my direction with her arm wrapped around Hope.

I smile wide and hold out my hand. "Hello, I'm Tina Cooper."

"Are you the babysitter? I thought Hope's babysitter was a retired school teacher." She scans me from head to toe and then frowns at her husband. He solemnly stares at me.

"Are you in high school? Do you live in the neighborhood?"

I glance back at her. High school? Do I look that young? I suppose someday I'll appreciate looking younger than I am, but it's still just an annoyance now.

"No to both actually. Ron should be back soon. He went into town to pick up pizza. I'll let him know you arrived." I pull out my phone. I still don't know which set of grandparents they are. They don't look like Ron, but that doesn't mean much.

"Ron? Shouldn't you call him Mr. Swanson or is respecting your elders no longer a thing for your generation?" His gruff disapproving voice reminds me of a professor I had in college. The man was always sour. I never saw him crack a smile.

I finish the text to Ron telling him Hope's grandparents have arrived and let him interpret that as he may. Perspiration dampens my back and I resist the urge to cool my body by fluttering my T-shirt.

How am I supposed to respond to that?

"Jay." His wife lays a hand on his arm. "We're Jay and Susan Summerfield, Ruth's parents." She stares at me as if searching for something.

Is she wondering if I know who Ruth is? Or maybe she just wants to make sure Ron is keeping her memory alive?

"It's nice to meet you. Hope talks about you both a great deal. I was her teacher this year."

There, now they know I'm not the babysitter or in high school.

"I see. Is it common for teachers around here to also babysit their students?"

So much for making it clear I'm not the babysitter. It's probably better if they do think it. Ron can sort it out with them later if he chooses to. Besides, I'm certainly not going to tell her I'm dating their former son-in-law. I smile at her. "Not that I know of, but it is a small town."

Hope's hand slips into mine. "Do you want to see the fairy village Miss Cooper and I built?"

Both their gazes lock onto our hands.

"Of course, pumpkin. Show me." Hope's grandmother holds out her hand to Hope.

Hope takes her hand with her free one and tugs mine with the other. As we walk back to the village under the trees, my phone buzzes. There's a text from Ron letting me know he's on his way.

Nothing else. I suppose it might be difficult for him to type some instructions on how I'm to handle his former in-laws, but I could really use some guidance.

Hope points out every detail of the village to her grandparents. To their credit, they show plenty of interest and enthusiasm for her creation.

I've been straining to hear any sound of Ron's return. There's a thud like the sound of a slamming car door. I stare at the house, willing for him to appear. A wilting sigh of relief whips through me when he walks around the corner carrying a pizza box. He didn't even bring it inside. Either he anticipated the tension between them and me or maybe he's worried about something else—like if I would tell them we are dating?

"Susan, Jay, this is a surprise. Why didn't you tell me you were coming for a visit?" He gives her a hug and a kiss on the cheek and shakes Jay's hand.

"If we did, it wouldn't be a surprise." Jay rocks back on his feet with his hands in his pants pockets.

"You've met Miss Cooper, Hope's teacher?"

So that's how he's handling this? I'm just his daughter's teacher.

"Yes, we were a bit surprised to learn her teacher is also her babysitter." Jay stares at Ron with a frown.

"Her mother is actually Hope's babysitter. Miss Cooper just fills in in a pinch."

And there's my cue. "Well, I'll leave you to your visit. It was nice meeting you Mr. and Mrs. Summerfield. Hope, I had so much fun building the fairy village with you."

"You're not staying for pizza?" Hope's face puckers as she stares up at me.

I wait a beat to see if Ron will intervene, but he remains silent. "Not this time." I give her a quick hug and then give the adults a wide berth as I stride towards the house at a fast clip.

"Ron, aren't you going to pay the babysitter?"

I cringe and pretend I didn't hear Jay's question. If Ron tries to pay me, I don't know what I'll do.

As soon as I turn the corner out of sight, I sprint to my car. How could he humiliate me like that? It's not like I expected him to make a declaration, but he didn't have to pass me off as the backup babysitter either.

I start the car and shove it into reverse. Couldn't he have introduced me as a family friend?

As I back out of the driveway and shift into drive, I spot Ron standing in front of the house. Had he really followed me to pay me?

I stomp on the gas and stare straight ahead.

The tears wind their way down my cheeks and I dash them away with the back of my hand.

Find the bright side. There's always a positive spin in a situation, right?

Hope. Hope is always the bright spot. She's such a sweetheart. Even if her father has suddenly morphed into a jerk.

I suppose nobody knowing we were dating could be considered a positive too. At least I won't have to explain or answer questions if we stop dating.

A sob squeezes my throat.

Is it over? Can we get past this?

My phone buzzes from the passenger seat where I tossed it. A text from Ron: *I'm sorry.*

I clamp a hand over my mouth to hold back the sobs.

I swore I wouldn't let another man humiliate me and make me feel like less than I am. Yet, here I am. Do I have doormat tattooed across my forehead?

I slap the steering wheel and then shake my stinging hand. *Dang it!*

At least it stopped the flow of tears. I scrub the remainder from my cheeks. I really don't want someone to spot me driving while crying and call my parents to ask what's wrong. Living in a small town has its downsides.

If Ron and I are going to move forward, we need to have a candid talk about exactly what we are to each other. I won't be someone's shameful secret.

I pull into my parents' driveway and park by the stairs to my apartment. I stare at the hood of my car with my hand on the door handle. Aren't I doing the same thing?

I haven't told anyone about him either. Am I a hypocrite?

How would I have introduced him if we came across someone I know? A friend? Probably.

But I don't have a child and I wasn't shocked with a surprise visit from my dead wife's rude parents.

I close my eyes and lean my head back against my seat. He could have handled it better, but he also could've handled it much worse.

Chapter Eleven

"**I**'m sorry. I was blindsided by them showing up here unannounced. I handled it badly." Ron lines up his silverware on either side of his plate for like the third or fourth time.

"I know. You've already apologized." Several times. Jack never apologized for anything, or if he did, he twisted it so I always ended up feeling like I needed to apologize to him for something he had done.

Ron called last night and left two voicemails before I felt up to answering his calls. The Summerfields stayed the night and then took Hope back to Cape Cod for a few days. After tossing and turning half the night, I accepted his invitation to dinner. We need to talk. I'm just not sure what to say.

"I must not be doing it right because you haven't forgiven me." He reaches over and takes my hand.

I give him a small smile and squeeze his hand. "Yes, I have."

"Then what's wrong?"

I push my salad around my plate with my fork. "I'm trying to figure out what to say without coming across as if I'm demanding ultimatums because that's not what I want."

"What do you want?"

"I want to know what this is." I lift our joined hands. "It's not like I expect you to make declarations to your in-laws or anything."

"Why not?"

"What?"

"Why don't you expect me to make declarations to them or anyone?"

"I don't know. I mean I didn't think you were ready. I don't want to pressure you."

He lifts my hand and kisses my knuckles. "I appreciate that, but you should expect me to treat you and our relationship with respect. I failed you yesterday. I have no excuse except I've known them since I was a teenager. They were my in-laws for years and I didn't want to hurt them by telling them I'm moving on from Ruth."

"Of course not."

"But that's not treating them with respect either. They're Hope's grandparents. They'll always be in my life. I don't want to be dishonest with them. Which is why I told them this morning that I was dating and met someone special. I didn't tell them it was you because I wanted to talk to you first and make sure it was okay with you. You hadn't seemed to want anyone to know, especially your family. And if I told them, then they were likely to discuss it where Hope would overhear. I prefer to be the one to tell Hope, but I won't if you're not comfortable yet."

That must have been a tough conversation. "How did they react?"

"Susan cried. It was hard, but they both understood and expected I would, eventually. I assured them they would always be an important part of my family."

"I'm sorry."

"For what?"

"Being the reason she cried. For putting you in that position."

Ron stares at our joined hands and rubs his thumb over mine in a soothing pattern. "You have nothing to apologize for. It was a necessary conversation because you're important to me. Our relationship is important."

"Thank you."

"You don't have to thank me either." He smiles and kisses the back of my hand. "You haven't touched your salad...except to rearrange it on your plate."

"Neither have you."

"Good point. Why don't we enjoy our meal?"

I nod and take a bite of the baby green salad with dried cranberries and walnuts. The tang of the dressing and the sweetness of the cranberries create a flavor explosion in my mouth. "This is delicious." I mumble the words around a mouthful of food.

Ron grins. "Wait until you try the rest of the courses."

"Did you cook all of it?"

He nods as he takes a bite of his salad.

Will he expect me to cook him a dinner like this? Will it be cheating if I get my mom to help?

When we finish the salads, he disappears into the kitchen and returns with the main meal. He places a plate in front of me and himself. "It's prosciutto wrapped chicken breast stuffed with spinach, mushrooms, and cheese with an asiago based sauce drizzled over the top. Then we have mashed potatoes and roasted brussels sprouts with a balsamic glaze."

I look at the scrumptious looking food and then at him. The brussels sprouts still sizzle and the warm scent from the chicken radiates from the plate. "Are you kidding with me or did you really make this? It looks like something I'd get in a restaurant."

"I've learned to enjoy cooking. I can show you all the dirty pots and pans if you like."

"I'll take your word for it." I slice off a piece of chicken and take a bite. It's so moist and flavorful, I actually close my eyes for a second. I point my empty fork at him. "Why have we been going to restaurants when you can cook like this?"

He throws his head back and laughs. "It's a recent development. Since Hope and I moved, I had to learn. Then I discovered not only do I like it, but I'm rather good at it too. I'll cook for you anytime you like."

"I thought my mother is a skilled cook, but this is spectacular." I shoot him a mock glare. "If you tell her I said you're a better cook than she is, I'll deny it and make you sorry."

He imitates zipping his lips closed and makes a cross over his heart.

After I've consumed two-thirds of my dinner, I realize Ron has stopped eating and is watching me with a slight smile on his face. I grab my napkin and wipe my mouth hoping I'm not wearing any of the delicious food I may have been overzealously stuffing in my mouth.

He's still watching me with that smile.

"What? Is there something on my face?"

"No, I'm just admiring your beauty—inside and out."

I blink while suddenly something feels lodged in my throat.

"We didn't finish our earlier conversation. I want to be sure we're on the same page. You're okay with people knowing we're dating...that we're a couple?"

I set my fork down and take a sip of wine. I flutter my eyelashes. "Ron, are you asking me to go steady?"

He laughs out loud and leans over and kisses me on the lips before sitting back in his chair. "Yes, I suppose I am. It does feel a bit like high school, doesn't it? Wondering if the girl will say yes. Should I have written it on paper and slid it across the table like we're passing notes in class?"

"We don't need to take it that far, but I wouldn't be opposed to a romantic note occasionally."

"Good to know." He picks up my hand and fiddles with my fingers. "You haven't said yes."

How is it possible this handsome, accomplished, charming, perfect, man is nervous and wondering if I'll say yes?

I stand and strut over to his chair. His gaze is locked on mine while I sit in his lap and loop my arms around his neck. "Yes, I would very much like to be a couple."

I initiate the kiss, but his hands grasp my waist and he quickly takes control. His tongue sweeps into my mouth and tangles with mine in a passion fueled dance.

My body melts against his. His arousal pushes against my hip and my fingers clench in his silky hair.

Will he stop this time too?

I don't want him to stop. I ache for him.

His hand squeezes my hip while his other presses my back closer to his chest. My breasts brush against him and my nipples become hardened points of sensitivity.

I gasp and shift closer.

Ron buries his mouth against my neck. His harsh breaths sound in my ear while his fingers clench and unclench against me.

"Don't stop," I whisper against his ear.

His body stiffens. "Are you sure? I don't want to pressure you into anything you're not ready for."

I drop my forehead to his shoulder. He's only been waiting for me to be ready? Heck, I was ready weeks ago.

"I'm sure."

He stands holding me in his arms and carries me down the hall to his bedroom.

I really should have brought that bag I packed and then left on my bed because I didn't want to seem presumptuous. When he told me Hope was away and invited me over, I couldn't help but wonder if he meant for this to happen.

He sets me on my feet next to his bed and pulls back the gray comforter and white sheets. I nibble on my lip as the doubts creep back in my head. What if I disappoint him?

He cups my face in his hands. "You can say no at any time."

"I don't want to. I'm just nervous. I want to please you."

He drops his forehead to mine. "You please me just by breathing." He places multiple lingering kisses on my lips. "I guarantee you have nothing to worry about."

"Okay."

He ducks his head and searches my gaze. "Okay?"

I give him a shy smile and lift my shirt over my head and let it fall to the floor.

His lips place tender kisses across my shoulder and down my chest. "So beautiful." He unbuttons the top couple of buttons on his shirt and then yanks it over his head before kissing his way across my other shoulder and gripping my hands in his. "You're perfect."

I slip my hands free and run them over his chest. Hairs tickle my palms and his warmth seeps into my skin. On tiptoes, I meld our mouths together.

The heat from his hands weave pathways over the sensitized skin of my back and front as he learns every nook and cranny of my body and what it likes. We remove our clothes in alternating fits of speed and lazy exploration.

By the time he lowers me to the bed and rises above me, both our chests heave with passion and excitement. This is what I've been waiting to experience—passion fueled anticipation on the edge of desperation and pure need.

His mouth replaces his hands in the exploration of my body. I swear my body literally vibrates with tension as I clutch his shoulders so hard I'm afraid I'll leave marks.

I swat at his nightstand searching for the condom he placed there earlier. I don't want to wait anymore.

Ron softly chuckles against my skin and stretches his arm past mine. "Is this what you're looking for?" He holds the plastic square between us.

I nod and bite my lower lip. His gaze latches onto the movement and he groans. "You really are perfect." His lips fuse with mine as the rustle of plastic and his shifting body makes my core weep.

Achingly slow, he fills me as he stares into my eyes like he's memorizing my face and this moment.

My breath and thoughts abandon me in pure sensation.

His body engulfs mine as his movements increase in speed. I clutch him to me and try to imprint the feeling in my mind so I never forget the exquisiteness, but the wave of orgasm crashes over me and I open my mouth in a silent scream.

I float along the river of sensation as Ron reaches his completion soon after. He places a trail of kisses across my face while he holds me close and our heartbeats pound together, chest to chest.

Chapter Twelve

The snick of the bathroom door closing drags me from the last remainder of sleep. I pry open my eyes and stare at the closed door. Light spills in from the part in the drapes at the window and casts a beacon of light across the opening. I roll over and glance at the empty space on the bed behind me and the indent on the pillow. I smooth my palm over the surface. It's still warm from his body.

I raise my hands above my head and point my toes in a long stretch with a smug smile on my face. The past night has erased any doubt in my mind if I suck at sex. I'm fantastic in bed—at least I am with Ron.

We must be running low on condoms. I swing my legs over, sit up on the edge of the bed, and open his nightstand drawer. An eight by ten framed photograph of Ruth lies on top. There's a faint outline on the top of the nightstand from where the picture usually sits. He must have removed it before I came over.

I suppose I should be thankful. It was courteous of him to put away his wife's picture before bringing me to his bed. It's not like I'm surprised. There are pictures of her all over the house. But those are family pictures.

This is just her. On his nightstand. By his bed.

If I *accidentally* drop the frame on the floor, the glass might break.

If I drop it from a higher height, it would be more likely. The broken glass might tear the picture. It's not out of the realm of possibility. I could help it along while trying to pick up the pieces.

The shower turns on in the bathroom.

I gently slide the drawer shut. I'm jealous of a dead woman.

How pathetic is that?

I pick up his blue T-shirt from the floor at the foot of the bed. I tossed it there after yanking it off him last night. We'd returned to the kitchen for dessert and clean up after the first time we made love. He'd worn this shirt. Burying my face in the material, I breathe deep. His unique scent still permeates the shirt. I pull it over my head and smooth it into place. The hem ends around mid thigh.

I wander down the hall to the kitchen. Coffee might clear my head. The coffee maker is already turned on with a cup waiting to be filled. Ron is ever efficient and courteous. If he were over my place, he'd probably have a hard time locating the coffee or a clean cup. I press the button and the machine whirs as the coffee brews. I prop my hip against the cabinets and fold my arms over my chest while I wait.

Ron and I are vastly different. He's neat. I'm messy. He cooks delicious healthy meals. I heat up leftover pizza in the microwave for breakfast. He has a calendar on the kitchen wall with all his and Hope's appointments. I have pieces of paper strewn about my car and purse that I always forget to put on the calendar in my phone.

But none of that bothers me the most.

The coffee sputters as it finishes filling the mug. I dump two packets of sugar and a healthy splash of half and half from the fridge into the cup and stir it slowly with a spoon, watching as it turns from black to a pale beige.

No, what worries me the most is that I'll always be second best.

He might make room in his heart for me and even come to love me as I already love him, but it'll never be the way he loves Ruth.

The sweet, hot coffee burns my tongue and I wince as tears fill my eyes. I press the tip of my tongue to the back of my teeth and squeeze my eyes shut until the tears dry up. I will not cry and spoil a perfect weekend.

Cradling my coffee in my hands, I wander into the living room after pausing in the hallway to listen to the shower still running. Ruth's smile mocks me from various pictures displayed around the room. If we get married someday, will he simply add pictures of me with him and Hope next to hers? Or will he remove at least some of them to make room for pictures of us as a family?

Am I the worst, selfish, bitch thinking this way? Is it wrong to feel like I'll always be competing and coming up short with a dead woman?

My hand shakes slightly as I gulp my coffee, not caring that it still scalds my throat as it goes down. My gaze darts around the room. She never lived in this house, but there are traces of her everywhere. A stack of photo albums line a lower shelf. I bet every single one is filled with pictures of Ruth.

My lips tremble. I have to get out of here before he finishes in the bathroom. He'll see my emotions written all over my face and then he'll want to talk about it, soothe me, and make things right.

I lunge for the kitchen and drop my cup in the sink. It wobbles wildly and falls to its side. Hopefully, it's not damaged or one of his favorites. Ruth probably purchased the damn mug for their home together.

Good, I hope it is broken. I could slowly break everything so that it needs to be replaced, fresh and new, with no residual memories attached.

My shorts are on the floor in front of the dresser. I yank them on while darting glances at the bathroom door.

No way can he see me like this. I can't possibly have a mature, coherent conversation with him about my insane jealousy or need to be first in his heart. Not now. Maybe never.

What would he think of me?

I jog down the hallway as silently as I can, jam my feet into my flats by the front door, and grab my purse off the coat hanger. The door creaks as I ease it open and I wince. Instead of opening it wider and risk more noise, I ease through the narrow opening and close it behind me.

He will think I'm a selfish, spoiled, immature, bitch that sneaks out without a word. I shove my hand in my purse searching for my keys. He will think I'm too young for him. He'll think he got off easy and found out what a mess I am before Hope got too attached.

My fingers close around my phone instead of my keys.

I can't just disappear without telling him something.

Snickers. I shoot him a text that I need to go home to take care of my cat and we'll talk later. I add an *I'm sorry* too.

The keys jab my finger as I stuff my phone back in my purse. I stare at his house the entire time I back out of the driveway. Miraculously, no one is coming and I don't plow over his mailbox.

He doesn't need to know that Mom or Dad always check on Snickers for me if I'll be away more than a few hours. He only knows that I texted my mom to let her know I wouldn't be home the night before. Typical, courteous, Ron asked if I needed to call my parents so they wouldn't worry if my car wasn't parked by the garage. I told him about the system my parents and I developed long ago where I send a short text letting them know I won't be coming home so they don't worry and they promise in exchange not to pepper me with questions about my whereabouts and with whom until later.

Hope comes home tomorrow. I can put him off with one excuse after another until then. He won't want to talk in front of her.

I brush my hair back from my cheek and my hand comes away wet. I stare at my damp hand for a second. I'm crying and I didn't even know it.

Have I just ruined our relationship before it really even got started?

Damn it! I grip the steering wheel tight and shake it with all my might. What is wrong with me? He's so perfect. Why can't it be enough? Why do I need more? Why do I have to be first? Why can't I just accept what he can give me?

My legs stick to the seat so I slap on the air conditioning as tears continue to pour down my face and neck.

Green lawns and trees pass by in a blur on either side of me. I let my foot off the gas and coast to the side of the road. I need to talk to someone before I totally screw up this relationship and damage it beyond all redemption. Who? Who will listen and give me an honest, unbiased opinion?

Not my parents. They don't know about Ron and they'll hardly be unbiased. Monica knows about Ron, but can I really spill all my deep, dark, secret terrors to her? She knows we've flirted. She might suspect we're dating now that school has ended, but we haven't talked about it.

It would be weird if I just called her unexpectedly and spouted off my dive into crazy Ville, wouldn't it?

Jen? My sister doesn't know about Ron, but she would absolutely tell me if I'm being unreasonable. Yes, she's likely to take my side, but she's never had a problem calling me on my bullshit either. I could use a dose of her reality check.

I execute a k-turn and drive back down the road to a small park with hiking trails about halfway between Ron's house and my parents'. Luckily, it's still early in the morning and only the dedicated hikers or mountain bikers are out. There's only three cars in the parking lot and not a person in sight.

Are you up? I send the text and watch for the blinking lights signaling a response.

Instead of a text, my phone rings and Jen's name appears. I push the button to answer and it transfers to my car speaker. "Hi."

"What are you doing up at this ungodly hour? It's Sunday."

"Sorry. I need some advice."

"Okay, let me have a shot of caffeine first."

I hear the pop of a top on a can and her swallowing. "Please tell me you're not drinking soda for breakfast?"

"Okay, I won't *Mom*, but what's the difference between the sugar and cream loaded coffee you drink and soda?"

"You probably have a valid point."

"Of course I do. Now, Dr. Jen is all ears and ready to impart some wisdom. Spill it."

"Ron Swanson and I are dating." I hold my breath waiting for her reaction.

"Duh. So?"

"Wait, you knew?"

"Please, of course, I knew. You two have been making googly eyes at each other for months."

"Googly eyes?"

"Yes, now what's the problem?"

"I'm jealous of his dead wife. We had a beautiful weekend together and then I woke up and found a picture of her he had obviously shoved into his nightstand when I came over and then I went a little insane and had a meltdown.”

“How did he react?”

“He didn’t see it. He was in the bathroom. I took off before he could.”

“Where are you now? Home?”

“No, I’m sitting in my car at Sunset Park.”

A text from Ron flashes on my phone screen. *Everything okay?* Followed by: *Are you coming back?*

I squeeze my eyes closed.

What sounds like slamming drawers echoes through my car. “Jen?”

“I’m getting dressed. I can be there in a half hour.”

“You don’t have to. Just tell me what to say to him. He’s texting me asking me if I’m okay and if I’m coming back.”

“You left without saying anything to him?”

“As I was leaving, I lied and texted him I had to take care of Snickers.” Dropping my head back on my shoulders, I squeeze my eyes shut. “I’m a terrible person.”

“Shut up. You are not.” The tap, tap, tap, of her running down the stairs sounds through my car. “Text him I called you and said I needed you and that you’ll call him later.”

“So I should lie some more?”

“Tina, I need you. There, it’s not a lie.”

“Very funny.”

“Do it.”

A door slams and she huffs a breath. “Listen I’m about to get in my car so it’ll be a second while the phone switches over to Bluetooth. Send him the text so he won’t worry. He seems like the worrying type.”

“Okay, he is.”

I send him the text. Dots appear a second before his response. *Call me if you need me.* Then, *And even if you don’t.*

I bounce my head against the steering wheel. *I am an awful person.*

“Hey, what’s that noise?”

I lift my head and mumble, “nothing.”

She sighs so loudly it sounds a bit like I’m in a wind tunnel. “Did you send the text?”

"Yes, he told me to call him if I need him and even if I don't."

"Sweet."

"Yes, he is."

A horn honks and Jen yells, "Calm your tits!"

"Please drive careful."

"I am. The light only turned green a second ago. People are so impatient."

"Says Miss Impatient herself."

"Yeah, yeah." She clucks her tongue. "You didn't run out of his house naked, did you? I think I might have a hoodie in the back somewhere, but that's about it. Do I need to stop along the way and grab you some clothes?"

"Thanks, but I had the sense enough to put on my shorts and his T-shirt." I lift the material and give it a sniff. Yup, it still carries his scent.

"Did you just sniff his shirt?"

I frown at my dashboard. How did she hear that and know what I was doing? "Maybe."

"Damn girl, you've got it so bad."

"Thanks for your pearls of wisdom, but I already knew that."

"Did you? I thought you called me because you were having doubts and you wanted my sage advice."

"I'm not having doubts about my feelings, only his."

"How long has his wife been gone?"

"Three years." The anniversary was in May. Hope told me they had a memorial at her grandparents' church.

"Are you the first woman he's dated?"

"He went on one date with a woman before they moved here." His friend pressured him into it and Ron said he hated every minute.

"So, you're the first woman he's been with and gotten serious about?"

"Yes."

"His feelings for you must be pretty strong then if he's made that step."

"I know Ron cares for me, but he's so clearly still in love with his wife—will always be in love with her. She was his high school sweetheart. They have a child together. They didn't get divorced, she died.

Her picture is everywhere in the house." I draw my legs up onto the seat and hug my knees to my chest. "I don't want to be second best with the man I love. I don't want to always wonder if he's comparing me to her and finding me lacking. I want him to be madly in love with me and only me. How do I get past feeling this way?"

"Why should you?"

"What do you mean?"

"I think it's perfectly natural to prefer to be the only woman he jerks off to. The only woman he has pictures on his nightstand of."

"Gee, Jen, not exactly the romantic way I would put it."

"That's what you have me for. Look, falling in love is all about taking a chance on someone, right? Trusting that they'll love you the way you want to be loved and not break your heart?"

"Yes."

"I've never met a guy I wanted to take that chance with, not a single one. Don't be me. I've always envied your positive attitude and trust in people."

"I trusted Jack and look where that got me."

"Jack is an asshole."

"True, but I didn't see it then."

"I did and I'm telling you Ron isn't an asshole. Tell him how you're feeling. Give him a chance."

"You think I should tell him I'm jealous of Ruth? Won't he think badly of me?"

"Why would he? Jealousy is normal. He was certainly jealous of Carter's friend hitting on you at the Memorial Day party."

"He was?"

"Yup, if his eyes were laser beams, that guy would have gone up in a puff of smoke."

I laugh. "I had no idea he knew Kevin was flirting with me, or that it bothered him. Although that was the day he first asked me out."

"Tell him how you feel, Sis."

A car pulls up next to me. Jen smiles and I smile back. Her hair is in a lopsided ponytail and yesterday's makeup is smudged under her eyes. We must look a frightful pair. I haven't looked in a mirror, but I can only guess my tear-stained face is red and splotchy and my hair probably looks like it hasn't been brushed in days. Sisterly love. Who else would drive out here to rescue me at the drop of a hat?

"You good?"

I nod and smile.

"You going home or back to Ron's?"

I bite my lip. She drove all the way over here.

"My vote is for Ron's."

"You don't mind? You drove all the way over here."

She rolls her eyes. "Please, this was nothing. Tammy once called me frantic in the middle of the night and insisted she was done with her boyfriend and needed a ride. I drove two hours only to find out they'd made up and she forgot to call me because they were having makeup sex."

"You're the best."

"I know it." She grins.

I grin back. "I'm going to Ron's."

Chapter Thirteen

nxiety fills my chest and tightens my throat as I pull into Ron's driveway. I have no way of predicting how this will end. I'm confident he'll be kind, but will he understand my point of view or think I'm crazy and unreasonable? *Am I being unreasonable?* I do feel a bit unhinged with all these chaotic thoughts scrambling my brain. I should've waited to have this conversation with him after I had time to work through all of it and know exactly what I want to say and how to say it.

The passenger door opens and I jump and let out a brief scream. Ron puts everything strewn across the passenger seat onto the dash, clears a path on the floor with his feet, and climbs into my car.

He scans my face. "You've been crying. Is your sister all right?"

Shame courses through me. Now he'll know I lied.

"She's fine. It was my emergency, not hers. I lied. I'm sorry."

"Talk to me, Tina. What's going on? I suppose having to leave and take care of Snickers was a lie too?"

I nod and rub my empty ear lobe between my fingers. Where did I leave my earrings? There are birds singing somewhere outside the car. I scan the trees, but there's no sign of them.

"I saw the picture of Ruth in your nightstand. I'm not a snoop or anything. I was looking for more condoms. By the line on top of the nightstand, I could tell that's where you normally keep it. Which, of course, is totally normal. She was your wife after all, and you love her—will always love her. I know that."

"Tina, please look at me."

I shake my head and continue to stare out the window. If I look at him now. I'll breakdown again.

"Before you say anything, I want you to know I realize how ridiculous it is that I'm so upset and jealous of her. I'm being unreasonable and probably immature. But I can't help it. It hurts."

The passenger opens and Ron climbs out of the car. *Oh my God!* He's so disgusted with me he's leaving without a word. What am I going to do? How do I fix this?

Panicked breaths stutter out of me while I grip the steering wheel so tight my knuckles turn white.

Instead of walking towards the house, he walks over, opens my door, and squats down so we're on eye level. He solemnly searches my face for a moment, for what, I have no idea.

He reaches in, picks me up, and then sits back down on my seat with me in his arms.

I burst into tears.

He wraps his arms tighter around me while I bury my face in his chest and blubber all over him.

My sobs slowly subside while he continues holding me and rubbing my back. His chin rests on top of my bent head.

"I'm so sorry I hurt you. You know how our brains tend to ignore things after a while? I don't look at the picture. I haven't in some time. I forgot it was even there until Susan pointed it out and mentioned it was one of her favorites. I took it down after that because it didn't seem right to leave it up, for your sake as well as my own. I can't promise to remove all pictures of her. She's still Hope's mother and I wouldn't want to erase her memory."

I raise my head. "I would never expect you to. I'm not that selfish, I promise."

Ron kisses me on the forehead. "I know you're not selfish. And I promise we'll figure out the right way to honor her and keep her memory alive for Hope while being respectful of your and my relationship as well. It was a careless oversight on my part. I promise you I'm not living in the past."

He cups my cheek in his hand. "I'm in love with you and I want to build a future with you. In order to make this work, we have to be honest with each other and talk when something is bothering us, okay? I don't want you disappearing—especially not taking off in a car and driving while you're upset. It's not safe."

"You're in love with me?" My chin wobbles, but I press my lips together. He doesn't need me soaking his shirt any more than I already have. *He loves me!*

"I love you too. And I'm so sorry. You're right, I shouldn't have driven off."

His wife died in a car accident. Why didn't I think of that?

A slow smile spreads across his face. "You love me too, huh?"

"Of course, I do! Why else would I act so insane?"

He chuckles, lowers his head, and kisses me.

I put my hand on his chest. "Ron, I'd like to clear the air completely. There are some things about me you should know. I don't want to worry that you'll discover them later and it will change the way you feel about me."

He frowns slightly and gets a perplexed expression on his face. "Okay."

I take a deep breath and blow it out. "I'm not a neat person. I can be kind of a slob actually, not like unhygienic or anything, but messy."

Ron lifts an eyebrow and smiles. "Honey, I'm sitting in your car."

So? I glance around at the papers, bags, accessories, and miscellaneous belongings strewn throughout my car. Oh, right, point taken.

"I don't mind cleaning. I'm rather good at organizing too." He glances over his shoulder at the interior of my car. "How about if I clean this out for you?"

"I don't enjoy cooking either. I can do the basics and stuff, but most of the time I'd much rather eat leftover pizza...cold."

"I think we've already established I can cook, but you can eat pizza anytime and at any temperature you like. We never finished our topping taste challenge."

I narrow my eyes and purse my lips. "I'm always late."

Ron chuckles. "If it's important for you to be on time, I'll tell you to be there a half hour earlier than you need to."

My lips twitch. "I tend to be impulsive."

"No kidding. It's a perfect foil to my boring predictability."

I rub his chest. "You're not boring or predictable. You're reliable. There's a significant difference."

Might as well go all in. I rest my hands in my lap. "I can be insecure."

"So can I. I'm ten years older than you. I worry you'll realize you don't want to be saddled with an old man with baggage."

"But that's ridiculous!"

"You're young with your whole life ahead of you. I'm a single dad who's fast approaching middle age."

"You're only thirty-five and Hope is the sweetest girl there is, any woman would love to be her mother. I mean...I don't mean I expect to be her mother. I know Ruth is her mother. I just meant..."

"I know what you meant and I love you for it. You must realize Hope loves you too."

"She loves me as her teacher, but how's she going to feel about us dating?" What if Hope is possessive of her father and gets upset at the thought of him dating someone? Will she resent me?

Ron laughs. "Hope has been dropping hints all year about you making some little girl a wonderful mommy and man a wife."

"She has?"

"I think she knew you were the one even before I did."

"Well, she is awful smart."

"That she is." He runs his finger along the V-neck of my shirt. My skin pebbles. "I really like you wearing my shirt."

"Oh." I glance down. "I forgot I was wearing it."

"I think you should wear my shirts more often." He tucks my hair behind my ear. "Any other worries dancing around in that beautiful head of yours?"

I shake my head. "Well, there is one..."

"Which is?"

I curve my arms around his neck and whisper in his ear, "are there any more condoms? Because I think we're going to need them."

ope's blonde head is next to Ron's brown one and the two of them are whispering. I smile and stop to watch them for a moment. We carved pumpkins today for Halloween. She chose a kitten for one and a castle on the other. Luckily, I found cutouts to use online.

"What are you two whispering about?"

Hope jumps off the chair and comes running over to me. "I told Daddy I want to put the pumpkins in the fairy village."

"You don't want them on the front stoop?"

She puts her hands behind her back and shakes her head. I glance over her head at Ron smiling fondly from the table.

"Sounds like a plan to me." He puts one jack-o'-lantern under each arm.

"Here, let me help." I step towards him, but Hope grabs my hand.

"I've got it." He stops at the slider to the deck. "Although, I could use some help with the door."

"I'll help, Daddy." Hope lets go of my hand and runs to open the door.

She skips out the door after him, but then runs back and grabs my hand.

The past few months have been idyllic. I fall more in love with Ron and Hope every day. When the new school year began, Hope had a tough time calling me Miss Cooper instead of Tina in school when she saw me, but we made a game of it. Granite Cove Elementary isn't my prison, it's my calling. I can't imagine not going to work there every day and seeing the wonder on a child's face as they discover something new which I showed them. Jack was wrong about many things but accusing me of being stuck and having no ambition was one of the biggest. My ambition is teaching young minds and I choose to do it here.

Why did I ever let his words make me doubt myself? If there's one thing I hope to teach Hope, it's for her to always believe in herself and never let anyone else tell her who she is.

Hope feels confident enough to ride the bus this year so Ron no longer drives her. Most days she'll stay after with me until I leave for the day and then we'll go over to their house together where Ron will make us dinner or brings home a pizza.

Ron sets the jack-o'-lanterns down under the tree in front of the fairy village. It's grown since that first day to almost encircle the tree. Hope and I planted flowers and now it looks like a true fairy garden.

Hope tugs on my hand as she dances ahead of me.

"What's the rush?"

Her face puckers and she slows to a walk.

I laugh. "Race you!"

I run towards the tree. Hope giggles behind me. I slow and allow her little legs to catch up. She plops down on the ground next to Ron. He laughs and grins up at me as she giggles against his side.

"We're all here, Daddy!"

"So we are."

I sit on the other side of Hope. "I think this was a great idea. The fairies are sure to love your creations."

"Is it time for Tina to light them, Daddy?"

"You want *me* to light them?"

Hope nods vigorously.

"It might be a little early. It's still daylight. The candles might not last long."

Ron clears his throat. "I put solar ones inside."

"Oh." I frown and look at Hope. "Well then, why don't you light them? It's just a switch, right?" I glance back at Ron.

"Um…" He stares down at the pumpkins.

"I want *you* to do it." Hope puts her hand on my arm and sends me a pleading look.

"Oh, okay, of course." I shift to my knees and lean over the pumpkin with a kitten.

"No! This one first." Hope pats the one with the castle.

"Okay." I shoot Ron a perplexed look and a half smile. I'm not sure what is going on here, but something is up. I stop before I lift the lid. "There's nothing alive that's going to jump out at me, is there?"

I can handle a prank, but no creepy critters please.

Hope places her hand over her mouth and giggles.

Ron makes a cross over his heart. "Promise."

I give them both my best stern teacher expression before lifting the lid and peering inside. There isn't a candle—fake or real. There is a tiny box. A tiny ring box if I'm not way off base.

My breaths get choppy as I beam at the box—frozen. What if I'm totally jumping to conclusions and it is something else entirely?

Hope's little face appears between me and the box as she peers inside and then up at me. "Aren't you going to open it?" She looks at Ron. "Why isn't she opening it, Daddy?"

"Um…I'm not sure. Hope, perhaps you should go inside for a few minutes."

"But I want to see!"

I come out of my stupor as Hope's face crumbles and worry is stamped all over Ron's face. I snatch the box out of the pumpkin. "It's okay!" There's a string of sticky orange attached to the box and I brush it away.

I force a trembling smile in their direction. Hope claps her hands and Ron shifts to one knee.

He takes my shaking hand in his. "Tina…"

"We want you to marry us!" Hope jumps up and down next to us.

Ron laughs. "Hope, remember how we talked about this and I said I needed to talk first?"

"Oh, sorry, Daddy."

Tears fill my eyes. He *is* asking me to marry him.

"Tina, I thank God everyday Hope and I moved to Granite Cove and found you. You put light and laughter back in our lives. I don't want to waste a single moment of our future together. I love you with all of my heart. You will make me the happiest man if you say you'll marry me."

I rapidly nod before he even finishes speaking.

Ron grins and pulls me into his arms as he stands. I half laugh and half cry as I hug him back.

"Me too! Me too!" Hope jumps up and down.

We open our arms and include her in the hug.

"See Daddy, I told you this was a good idea."

Ron shakes his head. "You certainly did."

Hope pulls away and drops down next to the jack-o'-lanterns. "See the kitten is for Snickers and the castle is for our house, cause you and Snickers will come live with us when you get married."

"They're perfect," I whisper against Ron's shoulder.

"Hope, can you run inside and get my phone? I think I left it on the counter."

"Okay." Hope runs toward the house.

"Is this really, okay? I know it's not romantic, but Hope was so excited and I was afraid she wouldn't be able to keep the secret any longer."

I shake my head. "No, no, this was perfect."

"You haven't opened the box and looked at the ring. Are you sure?"

I scrabble over the box clenched in my hand and snap open the lid. A perfect marquis diamond with clusters of smaller diamonds on the sides sparkle against the black velvet. I gasp and put my free hand over my mouth.

"If you don't like it…"

"I love it!"

Ron takes the ring out of the box and slides it on my finger.

"Daddy, I can't find your phone!" Hope shouts from the deck and we both laugh.

Ron pulls his phone out of his pocket and waves it in the air. "I found it!"

Hope comes running over. "Is it my turn?"

I glance at Ron and back to Hope. Her turn? Ron nods.

Hope smiles and takes my hand. "Is it okay if I call you Mommy?"

Tears flow freely down my face as I drop to my knees and wrap her in my arms. "I would love for you to call me, Mommy. And I'm so proud to call you, my daughter."

My heart overflows with love and happiness.

"I asked my mommy in heaven to send me a mommy down here, and she did!"

Ron places his hand on Hope's head. There are tears in his eyes. "She picked the best one for both of us."

I take his hand and give it a squeeze. Ruth helped shape the wonderful man Ron is today. Without her in their lives, Ron and Hope might have been quite different. She helped them become my two favorite people in the world. "She's a very special angel watching over us."

Thanks so much for reading *Whispers & Broken Promises*! If you enjoyed the story, please consider leaving a review.

Want a bonus epilogue? Click here or https://dl.bookfunnel.com/g8cz03bl2j

Other books in the Granite Cove Series (in order):
My First My Last My Only : Franny
Covet thy Neighbor : Olivia
No Choice At All : Rebecca
A Yearning Dilemma : Kelly
A Change in Perspective : Lucinda
Heart's Melody : Monica

. . .

To hear about upcoming releases, sign up for my newsletter: http://eepurl.com/dt5N7M

A Yearning Dilemma excerpt:

The door opens and my stomach plummets to my toes like I'm on a rollercoaster plunging down a terrifying drop.

What is he doing here?

Has he tracked me down after all this time?

No, that's not realistic. Is it?

He tilts back his black cowboy hat. Blond hair, the exact color of freshly made waffles, brushes his forehead. He holds a phone to his ear with a scowl on his too handsome face. A face that's been featured in multiple blockbuster movies over the past decade—not that I've seen a single one. If Holden Fox is in a movie, then I skip the movie.

"The answer is no. There's nothing to discuss." His gaze sweeps my store and lands on me. "I've got to hang."

My heart pounds in my ears and my throat is as dry as a desert. A sharp pinch stabs my finger.

Bollocks! I've stabbed myself with the needle. A drop of blood forms, and I stick my finger in my mouth before the blood can stain the fabric. How would I explain to Mrs. Roberts I ruined her blouse because I was too busy staring at Holden Fox?

"Is this the only store in town called Dress to Impress? Wait, this is Granite Cove, right?" He frowns down at his phone. "Did my GPS send me somewhere else?"

So he's not lost.

"You're in Granite Cove, and this is the only dress shop in town. Let alone the only one called Dress to Impress. I'm Kelly Tanner, the owner."

His gaze swings up to mine without a trace of recognition.

Of course he doesn't remember me. I was nothing but a momentary distraction to him.

Good, it's better this way.

He swaggers over to the counter in faded jeans and a tarnished, dented belt buckle.

"I was told to come here for my fitting, but it must be a mistake." His green gaze narrows as he scans the racks of clothes filling the store. He checks his phone and scowls.

The low, Texas drawl sends a shot of heat through my core, but I dump an enormous pitcher of ice on my traitorous hormones and grit my teeth.

Fitting? Please no. Fate couldn't be that cruel.

"H.A.? Mitch and Franny's wedding?" I hold my breath. Please say no.

"Yeah."

Why didn't Franny warn me? A simple heads-up Mitch's best man is a famous actor isn't too much to expect, is it?

"Then you're in the right place."

He looks around my store again and frowns.

Seriously, dude? My shop may not be the swanky, Rodeo Drive type of places he must be used to, but it's not some crappy hole-in-the-wall, either.

"If you'll follow me, I'll show you to a fitting room where you can try on the tux." I stalk around the counter toward the back of the store. Why did I tell Lenore she could have the day off today? I could be safely hidden in the backroom right now and leave her to deal with Mr. Hotshot Celebrity Too Good for My Small-Town Store. She may have never actually measured or fitted any of my wedding clients before, but I have trained her how. So what if this is the highest profile wedding I've ever done?

I snatch back the curtain on the dressing room I reserve for brides to accommodate the large trains or skirts and wave him in with a tight smile. "I'll bring out your tux."

A spicy scent reaches my nose as he glides past me and tosses his hat on the small table in the corner. I swivel away and stride to the backroom. What the heck does the A stand for? Arrogant? Ass? Actor? If Franny had said H.F. I might have put two and two together. Then again, probably not. It never occurred to me Franny's famous husband might have an equally famous best man. It should have.

I grab the tux and fold it over my arm. She could have warned me. When she handed over the measurements and said the best man couldn't arrive until right before the wedding, I should have asked more questions. Simply ensuring a qualified tailor took the measurements wasn't enough. I would have had forewarning.

I stop and take a deep breath in front of the door. He's just another customer. I've worked with plenty of celebrities at past jobs. He's nothing special. He clearly doesn't remember me. So I have nothing to worry about. He'll try on the tux and be out of my life once again. Hopefully, this time for good.

He's texting on his phone when I approach and doesn't look up even as I hang the tux on the hook inside the dressing room. "Let me know if you need anything."

The curtain rattles across the rod when I yank it closed and return to the counter. I put Mrs. Roberts' blouse on a shelf under the counter and drum my fingers on the countertop. I'll finish repairing the blouse once he leaves. It certainly wouldn't look good if I damaged her blouse after agreeing to fix the half a dozen garments she brought in. I should've directed her to the couple of local women who do an excellent job mending clothes like I do for anyone else that asks about repairing clothes. But, when she told me Franny referred her to me and hesitantly explained her eyes just weren't what they used to be and she couldn't see well enough to sew anymore, I couldn't say no.

The curtain slides open, and he steps out, frowning. "I told Mitch I have my own damn tux. This is a mess. Someone screwed up the measurements. Are you sure you brought me the right one?"

I straighten my spine and run my tongue over the inside of my teeth. The tux is clearly too large in several areas.

"I assure you, it's the correct tux. I ordered it based on the measurements provided." I march over, scanning him. "I'll retake your measurements. I can make the proper adjustments. You will have to come in for a final fitting."

"This was the final fitting."

"Correct, but normally I would have taken the measurements

myself. I went off the ones given as a courtesy. It is, of course, up to you. You're welcome to take the tux elsewhere for adjustments."

He scowls down. "I don't have time for this. I'll wear one of my own."

"Franny and Mitch chose this particular custom design. If you wear a standard tux, you won't match the rest of the marriage party and you'll disrupt their plans. Is that what you wish to do?"

I used to think his eyes were the exact same shade as the green stripe on my grandmother's antique chairs. But, as he glares down at me from his six-foot-three height, they're closer to the color of pond scum.

"Make it quick."

I grab the measuring tape from the small, hidden cupboard outside the dressing area and suck in a breath. He's just a customer. A rude, entitled one. I've dealt with plenty of those in the past.

The length of the pants and arms is perfect. I compare the new measurements to the ones I was given. "Have you lost weight recently?"

His gaze meets mine and darts away. "A bit."

He's probably slimming down for a new acting role or something.

"That would explain the difference."

Franny and Mitch's wedding is only a week away. I already have a full schedule. It's May and the wedding season is in full swing. If it weren't for Franny, I'd tell him to go elsewhere. She's one of the few genuine friendships I've made since moving to New Hampshire, and I don't want to disappoint her. I also owe her for the huge spike in business lately. Her and Mitch's celebrity wedding is a first for Granite Cove, and all the local businesses are seeing their sales skyrocket.

I scroll through my calendar, checking for a suitable time to schedule his fitting. Lenore will definitely handle that one. I'll go over every step with her beforehand. It should be fairly straightforward after I make the adjustments. She'll only have to bring him the tux to try on.

"I have an opening on Thursday morning at eleven o'clock. Will that work for you?" It dang well better.

He scowls as he taps on his phone. "Fine."

"You can change and leave the tux hanging up in the dressing room." I spin away.

"You'd probably get more male customers if you didn't have all these frou-frou decorations."

I slowly turn back. He's waving his hands around at the entire back of the store as he steps into the dressing room. I intentionally decorated this part of the store in a fairy-tale theme for my brides and other special occasion dress wearers. Yes, it is feminine. So are most of my clients.

Besides, it's not like it's over the top. The white-and-gold color scheme is elegant and tasteful. It's not hot pink or anything.

"Thank you so much for your unsolicited opinion. I'll be sure to redesign my store to suit your masculine comfort."

I yank the curtain closed so I don't have to see his too handsome face or the smirk spreading across it.

Get it here: A Yearning Dilemma

About the Author

Denise Carbo writes Romance and Women's Fiction. She is a voracious reader, loves to travel, is fascinated by the supernatural, and enjoys solving mysteries.

She lives in a small, picturesque, New England town with her high school sweetheart and their three amazing sons. Find out more at https://www.DeniseCarbo.com and sign up for her newsletter to be the first to read about sales, giveaways, new releases, and so much more! https://eepurl.com/dt5N7M

Cory soon discovers she is a witch and must learn to control her new-found powers. An ally, a confidant, and a surprise supporter guide her, but she is almost out of time. An immortal evil wants her powers and will stop at nothing to obtain them. When the battle lines are drawn, Cory must choose who is friend and who is enemy. Will love save her or endanger her even more?